Critical Praise for Marian Coe

Legacy
Marian Coe deliciously involved the reader.
Book Reader Reviews

Eve's Mountain
This well-crafted saga belongs in all fiction collections.
Library Journal

Coe's writing is straightforward, yet irresistible.
A master storyteller.
Midwest Book Reviews

Coe deftly weaves subplots of her characters into a
single intertwining strand, the result enjoyable.
Asheville Citizen-Times

Marvelous Secrets
Southern women navigate situations in flux in their lives
in Coe's gentle stories of choice and chance. In these
tales fate and choice enjoy a serendipitous synergy.
Publishers Weekly

Marian Coe has a native ability for writing stories
that immediately hook the reader's attention and
won't let go from first to last. *The Midwest Review*

[A] marvelous read. These stories reflect Marian Coe's
own wisdom and lively sense of adventure."
Author Lee Smith

(The stories offer) marvelous empowerment for women.
Joyce Dixon, *Southern Scribe Reviews*

Marian Coe writes with grace and vision of human hope
that runs like veins through time.
Book Reader Reviews

Coe's Sc   ) A Cot-
tage full   , finds
again a   herself.

Other Books by Marian Coe

Legacy

Eve's Mountain

Marvelous Secrets

Key To A Cottage

Once Upon a Different Time:

An Appalachian Adventure
Inspired by the Writings of
Charles Dudley Warner

by

Marian Coe

Illustrated by

Paul Zipperlin

High Country Publishers, Ltd

Boone, North Carolina
2004

High Country Publishers, Ltd
197 New Market Center, #135
Boone, North Carolina 28607
<http://www.highcountrypublishers.com>

e-mail: editor@highcountrypublishers.com

Library of Congress Cataloguing-in-Publication data

Coe, Marian.
  Once upon a different time : an Appalachian adventure inspired by the writings of Charles Dudley Warner /
by Marian Coe ;
illustrated by Paul Zipperlin.
      p. cm.
  ISBN 1-932158-53-7 (trade pbk. : alk. paper)
  1. Warner, Charles Dudley, 1829-1900—Fiction. 2. Appalachian Region, Southern—Fiction. 3. Asheville (N.C.)—Fiction.
4. Mountain life—Fiction. 5. Trail riding—Fiction.
6. Travelers—Fiction. 7. Authors—Fiction. 8. Horses—Fiction.
I. Zipperlin, Paul. II. Warner, Charles Dudley, 1829-1900. III. Title.
  PS3553.O345O53 2004
  813'.54—dc22

2004001236

First Printing July 2004
10 9 8 7 6 5 4 3 2 1

For Paul . . .

My Partner
In This, and All Things

Acknowledgments

As with all books, this one owes its existence and its presence in your hand at this moment to a coterie of extraordinary people, among whom are:

Barbara and Bob Ingalls,
who make writers' dreams come true;
especially to *Barbara* for her labor
in coding the quotes;

Paul Zipperlin,
my talented husband,
who provided the illustrations;

Judith Geary,
dedicated editor for this project;

schuyler kaufman,
who designed the text;

James Geary and *Russell Kaufman-Pace,*
whose skill and artistry enhanced
and placed the illustrations

and, most of all:

Charles Dudley Warner,
whose articles in the ATLANTIC MONTHLY of 1885
set me off on this journey.

Foreword

*I*n researching nineteenth century New England for a historical novel in progress, Southern novelist Marian Coe came across a detailed account of a party of Yankee travelers making their way south, on horseback, to Asheville. The year was 1884.

The report of their adventure was found in the yellowed pages of the 1885 famed Atlantic Monthly, "a magazine of literature, art and politics" whose contributors were "men of letters" from the time when Boston was the "Athens of America."

Charles Dudley Warner, the Atlantic Monthly scribe for this adventure, was a well-known travel writer and essayist of this time, reporting full details of the two-month trek from Abingdon, Virginia, through Tennessee valleys and rivers and over western North Carolina mountains, to reach the lively town of Asheville.

As a fiction writer, Marian Coe imagined the personal story of such a group of adventurers on horseback as they traveled together across the Southern highlands of over a hundred years ago. Visitors today have all the modern comforts as they roll through this natural beauty, now reshaped with highways and sanitized motels. Our intrepid travelers of the past rode through the land as it had been for eons. For creature comforts they depended on hospitality from taverns or those early local folks who would take them in.

The romantic plot and characters are entirely fictional; Marian Coe has borrowed freely of Warner's phraseology and expressions, because no modern writer could so accurately express the conditions and sensibilities of the 1880s. Those passages in which she most closely adapts Warner's words to her story are rendered in italics; quoted passages are formatted to evoke the original Atlantic Monthly articles.

Once Upon a Different Time

by

Marian Coe

June 15, 1884

Mr. Thomas Bailey Aldrich, Editor
The Atlantic Monthly
Magazine of Literature, Science, Art and Politics,
Boston, Massachusetts

Dear Sir,

I am honored you are pleased to accept the adventure story
I have proposed to render. Now that the war is twenty
years behind us, time may have mitigated feelings between
North and South. My journey should afford welcomed
information to New England's erudite readers. This scribe
is delighted my report will appear early in 1885 in your
prestigious pages. It is an honor to be included with such
Atlantic Monthly favorites as profound and witty essayist,
Dr. Oliver Wendell Holmes and fiction writer Henry
James.

My party of three leave soon to move southward on
horseback, seeking out no steam engine or stagecoach. We
will travel from Virginia through Tennessee and North
Carolina mountains all the way to Asheville, reputed to be
a summer watering place in the nature of Saratoga
Springs.

Each night I shall record impressions of scenery and

people experienced along the way. Once the travels are completed, I shall put together the complete report.

My party . . . includes a professor friend who rode for the North, a man of sixty who can ride and recite the tales of the Canterbury Pilgrims without missing a beat by reason of the trot. A third rider will be a lean young fellow, one born to the saddle, who will be our trailblazer. I do have a surveyors' information of the land we intend to travel; however, our guide has experienced tracking his native South as well as adventuring West. We set out end of July and should arrive in Asheville by early September.

Yours very truly,
Charles Dudley Warner,
ready to explore the hills, vales and mountains of the South.

Oxford, England,
July 20, 1884

Mr. Charles Dudley Warner
Boston, Massachusetts

My dear Cousin Charles,

I am now happily ensconced in my Oxford quarters, looking forward in the months ahead to the fine pleasure of total dedication to my studies. Yet, I have a distraction for which I must call on your help.

My betrothed, Lily Holbrook, has been writing impatient, inquiring notes from Newport, where she was to stay the summer. The restless girl has left that seaside resort to sojourn with her aunt in Abingdon, Virginia, whence, I fear, she will write more letters, disturbing my peace here. Only one solution presents itself. I depend on you, dear

Cousin, to take Lily along on your planned excursion. Thus, she will stay occupied and entertained, under your steady eye. I took the liberty of writing to her of your plans and invitation, knowing I can count on your doing this for me.

Do not fear. Lily rides well and she shall have a chaperone in her Aunt Tess, a sturdy female of past fifty who breeds horses on her own farm in Virginia. I have written to them, directing them to await your arrival at the hotel in Abingdon.

My apologies for this last minute request, but you see I must count on my noble Cousin, as my prospective Best Man, to provide this solution.

With grateful relief, I am
your busy Cousin,
Alvin

Charles Dudley Warner:
"The Friend of Humanity"

July 30, 1884

My Dear Alvin,

What do you leave me to say? It is too late to protest what you have set in place.

Knowing your preferences regarding the ladies, I am convinced, though I have never met her, that this Lily is a delicate beauty, trained in a New England school for proper young ladies. In this bachelor's experience, I have observed that such females excel more in the art of the coquette, plying dainty hands to embroidery or the piano.

It does not cheer me to know, Alvin, that your betrothed and her aunt are acquainted with the saddle. They are nevertheless females. Setting out on a manly venture, Lily, I am sure, will be as useful as a feather boa where rope is needed.

I am left in consternation; however, since you say these two will be waiting at the Abingdon Hotel, I have no gentleman's alternative but to meet them there.

Your dismayed and much-tried Cousin,
Charles

The Professor

Trail's Head

Abingdon, Virginia

On this fair August day, we gentlemen alighted the train in Abingdon, to be met by our guide for the trip – and our other traveling companions. We were glad to reach the hotel of promised comfort, even if we were to find two females awaiting us.

Young Starney, our local guide, with the help of a barefoot boy, led the horses around the back of the building to tether them. The Professor and I proceeded to the front porch. The flagging there was fully occupied by assorted *Superintendents of Affairs*, fellows tilted back in their cane bottomed chairs, dedicated to observing what was going on in town. At the moment, our arrival was the new sight.

My approach rated merely a glance, as just another lanky, dust-covered fellow of uncertain age.

Starney

The Professor drew the scrutiny, being short and rounded as a weathered tree stump, peering out from amid his bushy gray brows and clipped beard, confident as a judge. His leather vest over his barrel chest, his fine boots, and the way his felt derby sat on his curly white head, alerted the porch sitters that here was a city man. When he rumbled, "My good fellows, greetings from a traveler," they knew he was a Yankee at that.

They turned solemn faces back to their vigil of the dusty town street.

Before The Professor and I could enter the front door, out came a girl, wide skirt swinging above neat ankles in well-cut boots, her chin high, and an abundance of brown curls caught in a knitted snood bouncing at the nape of her neck. She made a quick path past us, down the steps, pretending not to notice the porch watchers who tipped their hats and halfrose from their chairs.

This would be Lily. We watched her waltz down the street ignoring the flutter she had just caused, or enjoying it.

Through the creaking door came a sturdy-bodied woman who could be just past fifty, and who could be the aunt chaperone. Arms crossed over her ample chest, she squinted past all to watch Lily whip down the middle of the dusty town street. Now she regarded us from a confident round face that had known a plethora of sun.

The Professor, who likes to be known by that formal title, introduced himself thus, while giving me the added accolade of *"the Friend of Humanity."* Yes, we were the two travelers beginning the horseback adventure.

She considered that, studying us over her halfglasses. "And I'm Tess Hartley, aunt and protector of that motherless Lily. I left Boston soon as the South came back into the Republic. You're looking at a Virginian now."

That announced, she informed us: "We've waited two days here. Now we must talk. When do we leave and where do we go first? I'm itching for a good long trek. Lily's horse is being shod down the street. She's gone to make sure they do it right."

Tess

I saw we had a Boston lady who had kept her Yankee penchant for speaking her mind.

Inside the worn front parlor, The Professor and I exchanged glances of agreed assessment. One could imagine this was a place of bygone bustle and mint julep hilarity. The place must be a fair example of Southern hotels of antebellum finery, now showing the deprivations of these years since the civil conflict.

We three settled in worn leather chairs. Now Tess wanted to know what each of us would be riding and who was accountable for knowing the trail.

"Here's our trailblazer," I said as Starney strode in, lifting his slouch hat to the lady, holding it against his middle as if he'd bowed, before sitting down. We watched Tess scrutinize this lean muscled young fellow, who wore with no explanation a mix of old blue and gray uniform, a Western scarf around his neck, his head of thick dark hair pulled tight, hanging back of his neck in an Indian braid.

"You know mountain trails?"

"Yes'm, first hand." Starney offered no more, his brown eyes sharp, but veiled beneath his sleepy look. In our few days with Starney, The Professor and I had already accepted that the boy was a lone-wolf, a silent one who did have a fine command with a horse.

I reported to Tess that I had an itinerary, furnished by a member of the coast survey, which gave us suggestions for our intended route, but that Starney knew the terrain first hand.

With Tess talking horses now, Starney sat up. His big black Rebel, he reported, was able to make any trail. The Professor was riding Laura Matilda, a short-gaited, good tempered roan mare, low to the ground, as The Professor's legs are short. My own legs being longer, I would be riding Jack, a steady chestnut gelding with a high wide back for my comfort.

Tess nodded. She explained proudly that she bred Morgan cross-bloods on her Abingdon Farms; she would be riding her favorite mare, Abby. "I'm coming along to shame my back from hurting," she admitted, rushing on to say she was hardy and needed a good trek, besides coming along with Lily, who had been at her place a week, tired of socializing at Newport. Lily had chosen Buttercup, a tough little cream-colored mare.

As we waited for Lily, The Professor asked chaperone Tess, in his Shakespearean tones, "Do we have a maiden never bold; of spirit so still and quiet, that her motion blushed at herself?"

Aunt Tess's pressed lips delivered her silent scorn. "You'll see."

With this going on, I made a decision: in my notes for the article, I would report our travels only for a group of two men and a guide, without mention of the women riders. I had no intention of bringing the name of my Cousin's betrothed into the public arena. No need to reveal my concern over including a determined young female and a chaperone who spoke her mind. The promised story was to be about the scenery, experiences and hospitality found, for readers' information.

Lily

Each night I should write my notes of the day's travel as planned. Any other experience I would save for some later day when seasoned males commiserated over their experiences of dealing with women.

Lily swept in, looking flushed. We men bounced up as she sank down into the old leather seat, her fine boots showing under the big skirt. I saw instantly The Professor would be entertained by the addition; but then, he was not responsible for the outcome. His eyes showed a grandfatherly gleam and appreciation of an added audience for his versifying. Starney stood like a wooden Indian before dropping back in his seat.

Lily's riding skirt was the divided kind, brought into vogue in recent years by the sharpshooter Annie Oakley. It looked like soft leather, obviously the work of a skilled seamstress who knew the latest modes for lady riders. The shirtwaist, while practical, did not hide the fact she was a fresh-bloomed maiden, the type one expected to find in a drawing room, perhaps displaying her skill at the piano.

"I wanted to go to Asheville," she announced in the pretty finishing school voice I also expected. "I have a dear friend from school in that town. She married a Southerner who took her down there. Left Boston for that! I must see how on earth she has survived this year later."

Starney sprang to his feet. "Your friend may have found there's a world beyond Boston." He walked out at that. He did not come back to hear our host call out that the supper bell rang close to sundown.

The Professor grinned, stroked his beard and quoted Walt Whitman:

"Earth! You seem to look for something at my hands,
Say, old top-knot, what do you want?"

He usually quotes Shakespeare, I told the room.

First night's report, written by fair lamplight . . .

Abingdon, Virginia, [is] prettily situated on rolling hills, a couple of thousand feet above the sea, with views of mountain peaks to the south, a cheerful, not too exciting place for a brief sojourn, yet hospitable and helpful to the stranger. . . .

The hotel, in front of which there is cultivated so much of what the Germans call *Sitzfleish*, is a fair type of the majority of Southern hotels and differs from the same class in the North, in being left a little more to run itself. The only information we obtained about it was from its porter at the train station who (promised) . . . "perfect satisfaction in every respect."

[We] found the statement highly colored. It was left to our imagination to conjecture how the big chambers with their gaping fireplaces might have looked when furnished and filled with gay company. . . . In our struggles with a porter to obtain the little items of soap, water, and towels, we were convinced we had arrived too late, and that for perfect satisfaction, we should have been here before the war. . . . [The item that would have pleased us most, had we been here earlier], was 'good lodging with clean sheets'.

Second night's report:
[The Professor and I looked about for any lively event to report.] We had dined – so much at least the public would expect of us – with a descendant of Pocahontas; we had assisted on Sunday morning at the dedication of the new brick Methodist church, the finest edifice in the region, a dedication that took a long time since the bishop would not proceed until money enough was raised in the open meeting to pay the balance due on it, – a religious act, though it did give the meeting a business-like aspect . . .

[W]e had been the light spots in the evening service at a most aristocratic church of color. . . . The sermon contained the usual vivid description of the last judgment, and I fancied that the congregation did not get the ordinary satisfaction out of it. Fashion had entered the fold, and the singing was mostly executed by a choir in the dusky gallery. . . .

THE ATLANTIC MONTHLY:
July, 1885

Monday's Start

The Professor grumbled himself awake. I found Starney waiting on the front porch where he had chosen to sleep the night, being the loner he is. I knocked on the ladies' door.

Peering out flushed and annoyed, Lily informed me, "I do not wish to start of a morning until I have attended to my preparations."

Behind her, Tess declared "We are appreciating a tub of water while we have it. On this journey I will not complain about bathing in stream or lake. Water is water." She sniffed elaborately. "I trust Starney allows himself the same facilities. Smells like his horse. Must we have such a fellow on the way?"

"Yes," I said with noble patience. "We must, as he is showing the way. This morning you are fortunate to have the time, ladies. *Virginia is one of those blessed regions where one can get a late breakfast, as it is almost impossible to get an early one.*"

Finally, as we gathered over biscuits and ham, I again endeavored to arrive at rules of conduct for the journey. We would be living on the country, trusting to the reported hospitality of the widely scattered inhabitants.

Lily swept in with a fresh, eager face, her brown curls obviously brushed strongly and tucked back in a snood. The ladies, I learned, each carry a carpetbag with feminine necessities, rolled up silk gowns, and romantic novels. I did not question the novels. The Professor came prepared with Shakespearean sonnets.

Starney sat alone at a table with his coffee and biscuits. I was relieved to see he was not charmed by Lily. He must have seen how she wiggles her dainty nose at his drawl when he does presume to offer a remark. My new concern was the possibility of a Rebel and Yankee war along the way.

The Professor proved to be the obstinate one on the subject of mountains, of which we have many upcoming. He declared, *"I maintain it's a man's right to not ascend one unless he wants."*

Did he look for a coy smile of approval from Lily? She was busy lacing her boot tighter. Tess shrugged ample shoulders.

As the trip leader, I said firmly to my old friend, "Professor, I personally believe in the value of being able to say, *'Yes I've climbed those slopes'* when the name of a mountain comes up in social conversation."

I confessed to Starney in private that it would take diplomacy to get The Professor over any considerable elevation. And the ladies? Time would tell.

Buttercup

Setting Off From Abingdon

This morning we five adventurers mounted up in front of the hotel, watched with studied interest by the porch-sitters. Starney stood by Lily, watching as she spread her saddle blanket, then her flat saddle, high on Buttercup's withers, and slid both down into place before tightening the girth.

Glancing at the Trailblazer, she declared, "You needn't help me, thank you."

From the porch, somebody yelled out, "That little gal knows how to handle her horse, fella."

Starney swung up onto his black Rebel, gave the sign, and off he went, Lily, Tess, The Professor, and I following him. Once out of town, we descended into the Holston River Valley.

Waiting for us were the Tennessee hills and conspicuous White Top Mountain, said to be 5,530 feet above sea level. Standing where the states of Virginia, Tennessee and North Carolina corner, that presence is a local celebrity. *We have been urged to ascend this mountain without fail. Already I had found that people recommend their mountains to others as they recommend patent medicines.*

At the start our horses were not ambitious. We went at an easy fox trot that permitted observation. With some relief I could see that the two females riding ahead did keep a good seat. The Professor sang out with some Shakespeare, his way of expressing jubilance, or to draw attention to his presence.

Soon, Lily's mare Buttercup became playful, dancing and capering. A glimpse of the young lady's face gave me the astonishing information that Lily appeared to enjoy this show of spirit; indeed, she almost seemed to encourage it.

Starney, with a quick glance backward, saw only the horse's antics. He slowed his pace to come alongside, reaching to grab the mare's bridle.

Lily raised her crop and slashed at his arm. "Don't you ever touch my horse!" she hissed.

Starney pulled his hand back quicker than he offered it.

Tess called out, "You damn near got hit there, Trailblazer. I told you Lily can handle Buttercup."

Starney cantered ahead, shouting back to Lily. "A good rider also has trail manners, Lady! You should be home at the piano." And off he went in a huff.

The Professor sent me a wry grin, knowing that this was as I feared: women's emotions.

Chaperone Aunt started singing an old ballad; the intention, I hoped, was to forestall further trouble.

We turned southward and descended into the Holston River Valley. Beyond lay the Tennessee hills and conspicuous White Top Mountain we have been urged to take.

The Professor shouted out his dissent at once *with a feeling that amounted to hostility. "I'll go nowhere I cannot ride. Climbing is the most unsatisfactory use to which a mountain can be put."*

Starney halted us without looking at Lily. *I have always believed in mountain-climbing as a theory, and for other people, though there is value in being able to claim to have ascended any high mountain about which one is questioned — since that is always the first one asked.* Discussion ensued among everyone but Lily, who stroked her Buttercup silently. *It seemed there was no way of agreement by compromise. It was finally agreed that no mountain under six thousand feet was worth the climb, and that disposed of White Top. Further, that any mountain over six thousand feet was too high to ascend on foot.* The Professor won. We agreed to forego the climb and ford the Holston waiting ahead.

This upper branch of the Tennessee proved to be a noble stream, broad, with a rocky bed and swift current. "We have Ramsay's to look forward to," I announced as encouragement. Someone had promised me that *Ramsey's was a royal place of entertainment,* in the usual manner of describing a lodging establishment.

The Professor sang out a version of Longfellow:

"Meanwhile impatient to mount and ride,
Booted and spurred with a heavy stride,
This Paul Revere is ready to ride,
To noble cuisine and a good bed to abide the night."

We crossed the Holston twice within a few miles. Riding horses across the fast-moving water became a ticklish business, except in the shallowest places. This whole region is full of swift streams, yet without a bridge to cross them.

We dismounted for a conference, and to eat the apples that practical Tess had brought from the hotel. We gazed around, wondering about the local inhabitants' having no bridge.

Starney nodded. *"Yep, getting over rivers and brooks and the dangers of ferries occupies the thoughts of most folks in a place like this."*

Lily looked dismayed. "Oh, what a hard life! Why would anyone stay in such a place, even if it is lovely?"

Looking at the sky, Starney said gruffly, "You can find hard life anywheres, but this place is home to these folks. I don't have one, but I can reckon how it would feel."

"Let's go see what's around the next bend," Tess said, again the brusque peacekeeper. We were off again.

The Holston River became the Laurel, according to my surveyor's maps, proving to be a most lovely rocky winding stream to be forded. The sun grew hot now, and Tess called out, "Where is this Ramsey's?"

"I propose," The Professor called out, *"that we pass the night there in the true abandon of plantation life."*

Starney reined in, pushed back his slouch hat, and ordered, "Hold up."

Lily wailed. "Trailblazer has led us the wrong way!"

"Nope, think we must've passed it."

"You mean that little settlement back there?" Indignant, Lily gathered her reins. "That old house, saw-mill and barn?" She dismounted, looped her reins around the branch of a nearby sapling, and drew a fancy cloth out of her carpetbag. She marched over to the stream, wet the cloth and held it against her face, turned skyward.

Tess dismounted, tying her mare beside Buttercup, and announced she would disappear for a bit "on the other side of the mountain" and that no one should take a step until she appeared again. She hustled off toward a grove of trees and brush, Lily marching behind her. We men took advantage of their absence. We assumed this would be custom for comfort stops during our travels.

We turned back to find Ramsey's.

At Ramsey's

Our two women travelers were most happy to find washing and bathing opportunities, and they enjoyed cheery conversation with the numerous children playing about the house and in the stream. Didn't see much of the husband, but our horses were well fed and glossy when they were led out to us in the morning.

All were bedded down now, as much as was possible at Ramsey's. Starney was on his bedroll on the porch. . . .

. . . So I write my report . . .

We soon turned southward and descended into the Holston River Valley. Beyond lay the Tennessee hills and conspicuous White-Top Mountain (5530 feet), which has a good deal of celebrity (standing where the states of Virginia, Tennessee and North Carolina corner), and had been pointed out to us at Abingdon. We had been urged . . . to ascend this mountain without fail. People recommend mountains to their friends as they do patent medicines. . . . The Professor expressed at once a feeling about mountain-climbing that amounted to hostility — he would go nowhere he could not ride. . . .

This whole region, full of swift streams, is without a bridge, and as consequence, getting over rivers and brooks and the dangers of ferries must occupy a prominent place in the thoughts of the inhabitants. The life necessarily has a 'frontier' quality all through, for there can be little solid advance in civilization in the uncertainties of a bridgeless condition. An open, pleasant valley, the Holston, but cultivation is more and more negligent and houses few and poor as we advance. . . .

Long before we reached [Ramsey's], the Holston river . . . [became] the Laurel, a most lovely rocky, winding stream we forded continually. . . . [We found Ramsey's] a neat log house of two lower rooms and a summer kitchen, quite the best of the class that we saw and the pleasant mistress made us welcome. Across the road and close to the Laurel, was the springhouse, the invariable adjunct to every well-to-do house in the region, and on the stony margin of the stream was set up a big cauldron for the family washing; and here, paddling in the shallow stream, while dinner was preparing, we established an intimacy with the family children playing in the shallow water and exchanged philosophical observations on life with an old negress who was dabbling clothes. What impressed this woman was the inequality in life. She jumped to the unwarranted conclusion that The Professor and The Friend were very rich, and spoke with asperity of the difficulty in getting shoes and tobacco. It was useless to point out to her that her *al fresco* life was singularly blessed and free from care and the happy lot of anyone who could loiter all day by this laughing stream, undisturbed by debt or ambition. Everybody about the place was barefooted except the mistress, including the comely daughter of eighteen who served our dinner in the kitchen. The dinner was abundant . . . hot biscuit, ham, pork and green beans, apple-sauce, blackberry preserves, cucumbers, coffee, plenty of milk, honey and apple and blackberry pie. Here was our first experience, and I may say new sensation, of 'honey on pie.' . . .

[The daughter] recommended it with enthusiasm and we evidently fell in her esteem as persons from an uncultivated society, when we declared our inexperience of 'honey on pie.'

'Where be you from?' [she asked.]

It turned out to be very good, and we have tried to introduce it in families since our return, with indifferent success. There did not seem to be in this family much curiosity about the world at large nor much stir of social life. The gayety of madame appeared to consist in an occasional visit to paw and maw and grandmaw, up the river a few miles, where she was raised.

THE ATLANTIC MONTHLY:
July, 1885

Off Again

Refreshed by honey and fodder and a night's sleep, we mounted up again. A saucy Lily said to Tess, loud enough for Starney not to miss, "I believe someone has discovered the pleasures of water. Probably after that daughter back there last night sneaked off from the kitchen to show somebody a fine Laurel pool."

"Well, be thankful for that," Aunt Tess said, giving Lily a warning look about any implied interest.

To The Professor, Starney said, louder than I've yet heard him speak, "I told you, a man can only hear faults from a Yankee female, specially spoiled rich ones."

The Professor chortled in his big chest and tried to come up with some lines about love and hate tied in a pretty knot.

As we made our way along, Starney agreed that it is difficult to say if the road ahead was laid out in the river or the river in the road. Today we crossed the stream twenty-seven times. Where the road does not run in the river, its bed is washed out and stony — tedious going.

Tonight I must write about this rhododendron beauty. The two female riders slowed, as did our guide just ahead, his back straight, head up, poised like a respectful Indian in this glowing summer heart of the woods.

Both ladies allowed that he might have been Daniel Boone at that moment.

"Do the ladies need to rest?" Starney asked loud enough for them to hear. "Shade coming up."

"Buttercup does, and so do my boots." Lily slipped down and loosened Buttercup's tack, pulled off the boots, pulled up the heavy divided skirt to her knees, and plunged her white legs and feet in cool water while her thirsty mare drank.

Tess started to object, then decided to do the same. We three men turned our backs to confer on the road situation, which I must record in my notes to-night. Silently we traveled on, toward the house where we would bed down.

Tonight, in this humble house, foregoing baths, grateful for apples and milk to balance greasy pork, we rest. What one pays is a pittance truly, so we make no complaints in the presence of our hosts. We take to our lumpy beds early.

Notes written under a smoky lamp . . .

[Today we] pilgrims went gaily along the musical Laurel as sun played upon rapids and illumined all the woody way.... The Professor soliloquized....

Five miles beyond Ramsey's [we crossed] the Tennessee line ... The Laurel became more rocky, swift, full of rapids, and the valley narrowed down to the riverway, with standing-room, however, for stately trees along the banks. The oaks, both black and white, were, as they had been all day, gigantic in size and splendid in foliage. There is a certain dignity in riding in such stately company ... [It presents] the impression of possible high adventure in a new world of such freshness. Nor was beauty wanting. The rhododendrons had, perhaps, a week ago reached their climax and now began to strew the water and the ground with their brilliant petals.... Great banks of pink and white covered the steep hillsides; the bending stems, ten to twenty feet high, hung their rich clusters over the river; avenues of glory ... [and] hues of romance wrenched exclamations of delight and wonder [out of us all, from] the Shakespearean sonneteer [to] his humble Friend....

As we picked our way along up the Laurel obliged for the most part to ride single-file, or, as the Professor expressed it, —

'Let me confess that we two must be twain,
Although our undivided loves are one ...'

THE ATLANTIC MONTHLY:
July, 1885

To Egger's

Starney always wandered off to sleep outside in the late night, but mornings, he would be waiting on the porch, ready to ride.

We were riding now toward Egger's, another hospitality promised as mighty tolerable from voices along the way, and our great expectation for the night. *Stopping at infrequent shanties on the road, with questions about the road ahead, we heard more about Egger's fine place. He is said to be the thriving man of the region, living in style in a big brick house.*

"If he thinks it's so fine," Tess said, sounding unsure for the first time, "Lily, we should have brought more gowns, fit for society. We have other tavern stops ahead."

Notes written at Egger's . . .

It was half past six, and we were tired and hungry, when the domain of Egger towered in sight,—a gaunt two-story structure of raw brick, unfinished, standing in a narrow intervale. We rode up to the gate, and asked a man who sat in the front door porch if this was Egger's, and if we could be accommodated for the night. . . .

This person, however, exhibited so much indifference to our company, he was such a hairy, unkempt man, and carried on his face, hands, and clothes so much more of the soil of the region than a prudent proprietor would divert from raising corn, that we set him aside as a poor relation, and asked for Mr. Egger. But the man, still without the least hospitable stir, admitted that that was the name he went by, and at length he advised us to 'lite' and hitch our horses, and set on the porch with him and enjoy the cool of the evening. The horses would be put up by and by, and in fact things generally would come round some time. This turned out to be the easy way of country. Mr. Egger was far from being inhospitable, but was in no hurry, and never had been in a hurry. He was not exactly a gentleman of the old school. He was better than that. He dated from the time when there were no schools at all, and he lived in that placid world which is without information and ideas. Mr. Egger showed his superiority by a total lack of curiosity about any other world.

The brick house, magnificent by comparison with other dwellings in this country, seemed, on nearer acquaintance, only a thin, crude shell of a house, half unfinished, with bare rooms, the plastering already discolored. In point of furnishing it had not yet reached the 'God Bless Our Home' stage, in crewel. In the narrow meadow, a strip of vivid green south of the house, ran a little stream . . . and over it was built the inevitable spring-house. A post, driven into the bank by the stream, supported a tin washbasin, and here we performed our ablutions. The traveler gets to like this freedom and primitive luxury.

The farm of Egger produces corn, wheat, grass, and

sheep; it is a good enough farm, ... The ridge back of the house, planted in corn, was as steep as the roof of the dwelling. It seemed incredible that it ever could have been ploughed, but the proprietor assured us that it was ploughed with mules and I judged that the harvesting must have been done by squirrels.

THE ATLANTIC MONTHLY:
July, 1885

Egger

Night Talk

I interrupted my writing to join the others outside in the moonlight. I said, *"Good honest people these, not unduly puffed up by the brick house, grubbing year after year just to survive."*

"The women at least," Lily fumed. "It seems Egger lets his wife and daughter do all the work." From what we observed tonight, that was true. "The daughter told me there was a neighborhood party now and then. And a church meeting once a fortnight, but that's all the socializing they have time for."

The Professor said, "Sorry, ladies, Egger lives in this placid world with no schools, no new ideas at all."

"Wait till a good schoolmarm moves in with new people and roads." This from Tess, who used to be a schoolmarm. "Children here will be awakened. I hope."

"I wonder," Lily said softly, "People look out on their own home with the eyes of habit. Coming to a different place like this makes me see my world is not the whole. How different would I be without the advantages I've known?"

Starney listened, said little. He took his bedroll to the porch and we would not see him until morning.

Resuming my report . . .

As time passed, and there was no sign of supper, the question became a burning one, and we went to explore the kitchen. No sign of it there. No fire in the cookstove.... Mrs. Egger and her comely young bare-foot daughter had still the milking to attend to, and supper must wait on other chores. It seemed easier to be Mr. Egger ... sit on the porch and meditate about the price of mules and prospect of a crop, than to be Mrs. Egger, whose work was not limited from sun to sun; who had, in fact a day's work to do after the menfolks had knocked off....

Long before supper was ready — nearly nine o'clock — we had nearly lost interest in eating. A wood-fire had been kindled in the sitting room, which contained a bed, an almanac, and some old copies of a newspaper. Meantime two other guests arrived, a couple of drovers from North Carolina, who brought into the circle ... the rich aroma of cattle and talk of the price of steers. As to politics, although a presidential campaign was raging elsewhere, Grover Cleveland a favorite, there was scarcely an echo of it here [around that fire.]

'This is Johnson County, Tennessee, strong Republican county, but doggone it,' Egger said, 'it's no use to vote. Our votes are overborne by the rest of the State. We got a Republican member of Congress, I've heard, but don't remember the fellow's name.'

[One of the drovers said] he didn't take much interest in such things, ... 'parties is pretty much all for office.' The Professor, who was traveling in [and espouses] the interest of Reform, couldn't wake a discussion out of such a state of mind.

Alas! The supper, served in a room dimly lighted with a smoky lamp, on a long table covered with oil cloth, was not of the sort to arouse the delayed and now gone appetite ... and yet it did not lack variety: Corn pone, (Indian meal stirred up with water and heated through), hot biscuits, slack baked, and livid, fried salt-pork swimming in grease, apple butter, pickled beets, onions and cucumbers raw. Yes, and coffee, so called, and buttermilk, sweet milk ... and pie.

[We privately agreed] this was not the pie of commerce but the pie of the country — two thick slabs of dough, with a squeezing of apple between. The profusion of the supper staggered the novices but the drovers attacked it as if such cooking were a common experience. [They, at least], did justice to the weary labors of Mrs. Egger.

Egger is prepared to entertain strangers, having several rooms with several beds in each, . . . the brick house magnificent by comparison to other dwellings in this country. . . . The beds in our chamber had each one sheet and the room otherwise gave one evidence of the modern spirits; for in one corner stood the fashionable aesthetic decoration of our Queen Anne drawing rooms, — the spinning wheel. Soothed by this concession to taste, we crowded in between the straw and the homemade blanket and sheet, and soon ceased to hear the barking of dogs and the horned encounters of the drovers' herd.

[We will depart in the morning] with more respect than regret. His total charge for the entertainment of [our party] and horses . . . was thirty cents for each individual, or ten cents for each meal and lodging.

THE ATLANTIC MONTHLY:
July, 1885

North Carolina

Our breakfast at Egger's was a close copy from the night before. We men were glad for the hot brew — the so-called coffee — with biscuits. Lily and her aunt stood out in the bright morning sharing the last of the apples with Buttercup and Abby. As we saddled up, Tess and Lily were still worrying themselves about the lives of daughter and wife within the brick house.

The Professor wondered if a squirrel had to harvest that steep slope, plowed by mules.

Starney looked around at what we were leaving, hillsides seamed with gullies. "Good soil here if it would stay in place. When land is cleared of trees, it begins to wash and muddies all the streams. Life was hard enough here before. Then with the war —"

"Through here?" Tess asked.

"War sickens a land even if the Yankee armies didn't march through here."

"How do you know about the war?" Lily demanded. It was the first time in two days she had directed a remark to him. "It's been so long over. You must have been a child then."

Starney's brown eyes darkened the way they can do. "What a boy sees at five can leave a stone in his heart his whole life long. Makes him want to run and keep on moving. I couldn't while Mama was alive needing me, but when she was gone I set out riding the country, seeing what people can do to each other and what war did to the South."

Lily's voice shook. "The North was hurt too. Not the land, but the men . . . in my family, in everyone's family."

"I know about the North," Starney growled. "Visiting Yankees don't know about the South."

I put in loudly, "Let's be about finding the forest beauty again."

Unfortunately, we kept seeing the denudation wherever the original forests were cut away for crops and timber.

As we trotted along, Lily offered with a heavy sigh, "I appreciated the springhouse at least."

Yes, in the narrow meadow, a strip of vivid green south of the house proved to be a little stream, fed by a copious spring, and over it was built the inevitable springhouse. A post, driven into the bank by the stream, supported a tin wash-basin and here we had performed our ablutions. I must report tonight that the traveler gets to like this freedom and primitive luxury.

Starney announced that this morning we were heading up Gentry Creek and over the Cut Laurel Gap into North Carolina. "That'll be Worth's, at Creston Post Office. Ready to ride?"

"Takes about fifteen miles according to my information," I offered.

"Expect twenty-two and a rough road," Starney

said. Then a gruff, self-conscious tone, "You women able to make it?'

Lily gave him a good glare. Tess shot her a reprimanding look and told Starney, "Able as you three. We'll let you know when it's time to rest beasts and bodies."

Off we went in a fresh new morning. Still in the environs of the settlement about Egger's, a young woman riding an old dappled roan joined the trail, waving to all of us, but trotting up front next to Starney.

I thought we should stop a bit in the fine shady spot ahead and visit, tell her we were collecting opinions of the country.

The Professor soliloquized: *"Here are feasts so solemn and rare...the scenery and young ladies riding through."*

We paused on the trail to talk. Lily eyed the girl's gloves with curiosity and respect. When she told us she was a schoolmistress in the county, her soft voice used standard English, with no accent of these parts.

As expected, her school room served the littlest children to some big ones — strapping boys — when the papas let them off farm work to attend.

"A school mistress," Tess said, pleased. "We were hoping there'd be fine girls like you bringing that advantage here."

We bade the girl goodbye and traveled on, up the steep and stony way toward a summit.

"Well, the beauty excuses the heat," Tess offered. "Good shady places here to rest a bit."

Lily dismounted quickly, to a grassy spot, her big skirt around her, and adjusted Buttercup's bridle to allow the mare to graze. We remarked on *the people we had encountered this morning with no peculiarity of speech. Novelists had led us to believe something different.* I commented that I must note that observation in my report.

Lily perked up, making sure Starney heard, "While some Southerners don't take the trouble to pronounce a word a visitor can understand."

Starney's drawl took on a crisp note. "Same as Yankees and New York folks who think the way they talk was decreed by God Himself. Anything else means ignorant."

Lily fired back, "For your information, though I do know how to play a piano, and I also speak my mind. New England females are taught that's our right, even if men don't believe it and get huffy to hear it."

Tess sighed with her chaperone frown, which by now I appreciated. I depended on her keeping the peace if we were to have a Rebel-Yankee conflict among us, bristling under the surface, threatening to explode into a war. No good calling for cooperation on this trip. I came expecting the pleasure of exploring and discovery.

"We're heading to the hospitable dwelling of a

colonel famous in these parts," I called out the encouragement.

"Ah, another fine promise — with what relation to reality?" The Professor responded.

We single filed over steep and stony Cut Laurel Gap under hot sun, heading for the summit, all of us silent with our own thoughts.

Tonight's notes . . .

The road over Cut Laurel Gap was very steep and stony, the thermometer mounted up to 80, and notwithstanding the beauty of the way the ride became tedious before we reached the summit. On the summit is the dwelling and distillery of a colonel famous in these parts. We stopped at the house for a glass of milk; the colonel was absent, and while the woman in charge went for it, we sat on the veranda and conversed with a young lady, tall, gent [elegant], well favored, and communicative, who leaned in the doorway.

'Yes, this house stands on the line. Where you sit you are in Tennessee; I'm in North Carolina.'

'Do you live here?'

'Law, no; I'm just staying a little while at the colonel's. I live over the mountain here, three miles from Taylorsville. I thought I'd be where I could step into North Carolina easy.'

'How's that?' [we asked, meaning 'Why?']

'Well, they wanted me to go before the grand jury and testify about some pistol-shooting down by our house,

— some friends of mine got into a little difficulty, — and I didn't want to. I never has no difficulty with nobody, never says nothing about nobody, has nothing against nobody, and I reckon nobody has nothing against me.'

'Did you come alone?'

'Why, of course. I come across the mountain by a path through the woods. That's nothing.'

A discreet, pleasant, pretty girl. This surely must be the Esmeralda who lives in these mountains, and adorns low life by her virgin purity and sentiment. As she talked on, she turned from time to time to the fireplace behind her and discharged a dark fluid from her pretty lips with accuracy of aim, and with a nonchalance that was not assumed, but belongs to our free-born American girls. I cannot tell why this habit of hers (which is no worse than the sister habit of 'dipping') should take her out of the romantic setting that her face and figure placed her in; but somehow we felt inclined to ride on further for our [backwoods] heroine.

'And yet,' said the Professor, as we left the site of the colonel's thriving distillery . . . 'To my mind, . . . the incident has Homeric elements. The Greeks would have looked at it in a large, legendary way. Here is Helen, strong and lithe of limb, ox-eyed, courageous, but woman-hearted and love-inspiring, contended for by all the braves and daring moonshiners of Cut Laurel Gap, pursued by the gallants of two States, the prize of a border warfare of Bowie knives and revolvers. This Helen, magnanimous as attractive, is the witness of a pistol difficulty on her behalf, and when wanted by the areopagus, that she may neither implicate a lover nor or punish an enemy (having nothing, this noble type of her sex, against nobody), skips away to Mount Ida, and there, under the aegis of the flag of her country, in a Licenced Distillery, stands with one slender foot in Tennessee and the other in North Carolina' —

'Like the figure of the Republic itself, superior to state sovereignty,' [I offered as] The Friend of Humanity. . . .

'I beg your pardon,' said the Professor, . . . 'I was quite able to get the woman out of that position without the aid of a metaphor. It is a large and Greek idea, that of standing in two mighty States, superior to law, . . . ready to transfer her agile body to either State on the approach of messengers of the court; and I'll be hanged if I didn't think that her nonchalant rumination of the weed, combined with her lofty attitude, added something to the picture.'

[I replied, I] even held in abeyance judgment on the practice of 'dipping;' but when it came to chewing, gum was far as [I] could go as an allowance for [habits of] the fair sex.

THE ATLANTIC MONTHLY:
July, 1885

New Morning
In the Mountains

*O*h, the pleasure of taking one's ease on the long shaded porch looking out on rolling North Carolina's mountains. Lily reappeared in the pretty dress from her carpetbag. She commandeered the hammock at one end of the veranda and presented a lovely picture of total submission to its woven shape; Tess was enjoying their room; Starney was absent.

But by noon we watched Lily out on the lawn walking swiftly away from Starney. Starney strode across the front grounds, deep in his own thoughts. We agreed that Lily must have triggered that private hurt of his. But now it was time to move on.

From the Colonel's, we descended into the country, fording streams again. Worth's, a trading center of the region, being our next destination. I made The Professor stay well ahead of me to keep Laura Matilda from throwing half of the stream upon this slower rider. I couldn't tell if there was any conversation among the three splashing ahead of him.

Our path delivered a panorama of beauty — charming open glades of the river, refreshing great forests of oak and chestnut, and banks of rhododendrons.

Lily called a halt so that the ladies could "go to the other side of the mountain." They walked off, and we men took advantage of the opportunity to dismount for a moment, too.

A sudden scream echoed through the laurel, and we hastily adjusted our clothing. We rushed around the bushes and hesitated just out of sight. "What is it?" Starney shouted.

"You'd best come look!" Tess called.

We hastened around the bushes to see Lily pushing her away, staring fixedly at a rope hanging from a tree. A rope with a loop for a head. A rope obviously from a hanging of the past. The shoes underneath had almost molded away. Lily screamed again. Starney came running, pushing Tess out of the way. I took Tess's arm and we both backed up, seeing the two of them face off. It was a scene in which I wanted no role. But I heard it all.

Just as quick she turned her angry tears on Starney. "See what the South did to slaves and people trying to run away? Your people. This horrible way of murder?"

Starney took her shoulders and said directly into her face, "Yes, that's a hanging rope. A killing rope. You don't know that Northern bushwhackers used them, too? Hordes of them moved through the South, claiming to be Union soldiers — but they were scavengers, taking advantage of the defeated countryside. A pack of three men or more could do it, aim their rifles on anyone who tried to stop them. Claimed it was a lesson to stupid locals for their treatment of slaves."

"How do you know?" Lily flared back.

Starney let go of her shoulders. He was too quiet until he told her, hissed it out like pain. "I saw what neighbor men brought in that had been my papa. They cut him down when the bushwhackers left. They brought him home. I was five."

Silently, somberly, we all mounted and rode on. On a shady path through all the color, Lily called out "Halt!" as if she were leading this party. She dismounted, handing her reins to her aunt, and took off toward the river bank to drop onto the grass there.

Aunt Tess dismounted, looped both mares' reins around a bough and followed in a huff of concern. Starney stood by his horse, looking again like a stern Indian. The Professor and I — both helpless males in view of feminine histrionics — dismounted too. Starney kicked dirt and stroked his horse's strong black neck.

The Professor emoted to the surroundings while I waited, concentrating on the blooms and welcomed breeze.

The quiet pause on the river bank must have served a purpose. The two women made their way back to the path with set, satisfied smiles.

But not yet ready to mount. Lily tromped over to Starney, and in a high, schoolgirl recitation voice she said, "Starney, I must apologize for assuming what to believe about your people, with no understanding of your feelings." She stood there, looking at him, apparently expecting an answer.

He nodded once, silently.

Lily stamped her little, booted foot. "If you had any manners, you'd return the apology." She turned on her heel and stalked away, looking like a gathering mountain thunderstorm.

We all mounted. I pulled Tess aside to say privately, "We must talk, you and I, sometime tonight. About Lily." She gave me a serious nod, and continued on the descending trail until we began fording streams again.

In the afternoon, we emerged into a wide open farming intervale, a pleasant place of meadows and streams and decent dwellings. Just ahead was Worth's, the training center of the region, post office, a sawmill, a big country store, and the dwelling of the proprietor. It cheered our hearts — the house looked not unlike a roomy New England country home.

Notes in the evening . . .

[Arriving here took us through lovely country.] How charming the open glades of the river, how refreshing the great forests of oak and chestnut, a panorama of beauty, with banks of rhododendrons, now intermingled with the lighter pink and white of the laurel. In this region, rhododendron is called laurel and the laurel (the sheep-laurel of New England) is called ivy. . . .

At Worth's, . . . we emerged into a wide, open farming intervale, a pleasant place of meadows and streams and decent dwellings. Worth's is the trading centre of the region, has a post-office and sawmill and a big country store; and the dwelling of the proprietor is not unlike a roomy New England country-house. Worth's has been immemorially a stopping place in a region where places of accommodation are few. [We found the proprietor of the hospitable home] an elderly man whose reminiscences were long ante-bellum, has seen the world grow up about him, [with himself] the honored and just centre of it, and a family come up into the modern notions of life. [The daughters and nieces] have a boarding-school education [from Stonewall Jackson Institute in Abingdon] and glimpses of city life and foreign travel. . . .

Our travelers are not apt to be surprised at anything in American life, but they did not expect to find a house in this region with two pianos and a bevy of young ladies, whose clothes are certainly not made on Cut Laurel Gap, and . . . books [about the house]. . . . I fancy that nothing but tradition and a remaining Southern hospitality could induce this private family to suffer the incursions of the wayfaring man.

THE ATLANTIC MONTHLY:
July, 1885

Worth's Fine Hospitality

$\mathcal{I}$ went looking for Tess this morning but found The Professor up earlier than usual, waiting for me in a pleasant chamber set apart for guests. He held up a copy of Porter's *Elements of Moral Science*.

I agreed, *where you see Porter's book, it's a sure sign there will be plenty of water, and towels too.*

I watched Lily, wearing her pretty dress, sitting with the young daughters and some other guests in the drawing room. Lily was reading aloud from a novel.

As she tipped the book to catch the light from the window, the sun reflected from the bracelet on her arm, doubtless the obligatory betrothal gift from Cousin Alvin. I wondered that I had not seen it before, but surely it was packed in her luggage against the rigors of the trip.

Here was my opportunity to question our stalwart chaperone. I found her on the far end of the veranda. She did not wait for me to ask, which I appreciated. I sat back and let her tell me.

"I thought it best she make amends by declaring her apology. You saw that yesterday. It didn't help what had already happened."

I was thinking: Cousin Alvin, look what you've left me, you over there in Oxford, lost in your books.

"Last night, Lily finally let me know what else has happened between them. I tell you, being a strong-minded, clear-eyed chaperone is no guarantee against young male and female trouble."

"Go on."

Telling me this, Tess was biting her lip. "When Lily dropped to the ground and covered her face, and I went to comfort her, she talked to me."

"'Just think, Aunt Tess,' she'd said, 'I accused him and his people with the same sins as those drunken bushwhackers who killed his own father.'"

Tess gave me a long sad look. "So I told her, 'You did it in all innocence. Go tell him you feel you've done the most callous, horrible thing.' She tried to tell him today she's not what he thinks. You saw how well that helped."

That night, at the fine dinner table, I watched Starney and Lily carefully not looking at one another. Everyone else was enjoying good talk and decent food, laughing politely at The Professor's expounding, and calling me The Friend of Humanity.

He even remarked, "Our young couple here are settling their own Yankee-Rebel war — we hope." His big laugh meant to brush the whole subject with good humor. It didn't help those of us who knew better.

Starney made a point of being pleasant to the three Southern daughters.

A silent Lily ate daintily like an ignored child.

Report the next night . . .

There is no landscape in the world that is agreeable after two days of rusty bacon and slack biscuit.

'How lovely this would be,' exclaimed the Professor, 'if it had a background of beef-steak and coffee!'

We were riding along the west fork of the Laurel distinguished locally as Three Top Creek, — or rather, we were riding in it, crossing it thirty-one times within six miles; . . . to Elk Cross Roads, our next destination. . . . We looked forward to a sweet place of repose from the noontide heat. Alas! Elk Cross was a dirty grocery-store encumbered with dry-goods boxes, fly-blown goods, flies, loafers. In reply to our inquiry, we were told that they had nothing to eat for us, and not a grain of feed for the horses. But there was a man a mile further on, who was well to do, and had stores of food, — old man Tatem would treat us in bang-up style. The difficulty getting feed for horses was chronic all through the journey.

The last corn crop had failed, the new oats and corn had not come in, and the country was literally barren. We had noticed all along that hens were taking a vacation, and that chickens were not put forward as a article of diet.

We were unable when we reached the residence of old man Tatem, to imagine how the local superstition of his wealth arose. His house is of logs with two rooms, a kitchen and a spare room, with a low loft accessible by a ladder at the side of the chimney. The chimney is a huge construction of stone, separating the two parts of the house built against it. . . . The proprietor sat in a little railed veranda. These Southern verandas give an air to the meanest dwelling, and they are much used; . . . The old man Tatem did not welcome us with enthusiasm; he had no corn, — these were hard times. He looked like hard times, grizzled times, dirty times. It seemed time out of mind since he had seen comb or razor . . . and although the lovely New River . . . was in sight across the meadow, there was no evidence he had ever made acquaintance with its cleansing waters. As to corn, the necessities of the case and pay being dwelt on, perhaps he could find a dozen ears. A dozen small ears he did find, and we trust that the horses found them.

We took a family dinner with the old man in the kitchen, . . . a meal that the host seemed to enjoy, but which we could not make much of, except the milk; that was good. A painful meal on the whole, owing to the presence of a grown-up daughter with a graveyard cough . . . Poor girl! just dying of 'a misery.'

In the spare room were two beds; the walls were decorated with the gay-colored pictures of patent-medicine advertisements — a favorite art adornment of the region; . . . old man Tatem was a thrifty and provident man. On the hearth in this best room — as ornament or *memento mori* — were a couple of marble gravestones . . . mounted on bases ready for use except the lettering. These may not have been so mournful and significant as they looked, nor the evidence of simple, humble faith; they may have been taken in for a debt. But as parlor ornaments they had a fascination which we could not escape. . . .

[In the] afternoon, . . . we meditated on the grim, unrelieved sort of life of our host. The Professor said, 'Judging by [the evidence in the cabin], he will charge us smartly for the few nubbins of corn and the milk.' The [evidence] did not deceive us; the charge was one dollar. At this rate it would have broken us to have tarried with old man Tatem over night.

THE ATLANTIC MONTHLY:
July, 1885

Watauga Forest

e left Tatem's with no regret, climbed the sandy hill and soon entered into fine stretches of forest, under the shade of great oaks. Starney called out the way, leading us over the hills to the higher levels of Watauga County. He was not to be seen last night, to report this in advance.

Off we went toward Boone. Every word of information we heard promised that Boone, the seat of Watauga County, would be the center of interest. So far on our journey we had been hemmed in by low hills and without any distant or mountain outlooks. The oppressive heat seemed out of place at the elevation of over two thousand feet. *One of the guide boards on the steep road proclaimed:*

BOONE -10M

if one took the right fork.

Another sign advising those who would turn left was written backward:

M01 -ENOOB

An ascending road of nine miles led us through open unfenced forest. Before sundown, we were riding into this capital's single street that wanders over gentle hills. We trotted past a gaunt shaky courthouse and jail, a store and two taverns. The Professor called out, "Stop at the most likely looking one."

We tied up at the tavern that we hoped had fair rooms and food, went in and presented ourselves. Five weary souls had expected cool air at 3250 feet, but the thermometer stood at 85.

At dinner, hanging flappers swept the length of the table. Tess said, "Look at that. Flies would carry off the food if weren't for those things."

We three men were surprised to find there were no refreshments available such as milk punch or rum or product from mountain stills. It was agreed I should include in my report, "the traveler must bring along his own poison with him."

Lily and Aunt Tess disappeared toward their rooms. Something was missing about Lily — her usual bright repartee, her saucy remarks directed to The Professor and meant for Starney. The girl was too quiet to be natural.

Later, I went out to sit on side steps to take in the cool air and watch the local folks. Here was Lily sitting in the dusky night alone. Sobbing — audible proof of what I had feared about bringing women along. Female emotions can put this practical, well-meaning male at a loss.

I sat down beside her. After all, this lady was supposed to be an in-law of mine by next year. "Lily, I miss the original, cheery confident self who started out on this trip."

She looked up with a teary face. "I wasn't cheery, didn't you know? I was fussy for reasons." At that she went into a fresh wave of angry tears. "You don't know a thing about women's feelings. Oh, go away. I'll try to stuff myself back into . . . whatever I was . . . "

I offered to stay another night in Boone so she could get more rest, or look around at the locals, but that only elicited, "See, you don't understand. You both see only the factual surface of things. That leaves out understanding a woman's heart and mind."

I murmured something about how travel to new sights can disturb old precepts.

"You may never have spoken a truer word," she sighed.

Notes written late in Boone, while The Professor snores . . .

Boone was 3250 feet above Albemarle Sound, and believed by its inhabitants to be the highest village east of the Rocky Mountains. The Professor said that 'It might be so, but it was a God-forsaken place.' Its Inhabitants number perhaps 250, a few of them colored.... The two taverns are needed to accommodate the judges and lawyers and their clients during the sessions of the court. The court is the only excitement and the only amusement. It is the event from which other events date. Everybody in the county knows exactly when court sits, and when court breaks. During the session, the whole county is practically in Boone, men, women, children. They camp there, they attend the trials, they take sides; half of them, perhaps, are witnesses, for the region is litigious, and neighborhood quarrels are entered into with spirit. To be fond of lawsuits seems a characteristic of isolated people in new conditions. The early settlers of New England were.

Notwithstanding the elevation of Boone, which insured a pure air, the after-noon temperature stood at from 85° near 89°. The flies enjoyed it. How they swarmed in this tavern! ... The mountain regions of North Carolina are free from mosquitoes, but the fly has settled there, and is the universal scourge.

This tavern, one end of which was a store, had a veranda in front, and a back gallery, where there were evidences of female refinement in pots of plants and flowers. The landlord kept the tavern very much as a hostler would, but we had to make a note in his favor that he had never heard of a milk punch. And it might as well be said here, for it will have to be insisted on later, that the traveler, who has read about illicit stills till his imagination dwells upon the indulgence of his vitiated tastes of the mountains of North Carolina, is doomed to disappointment. If he wants to make himself an exception to the sober people whose cooking will make him long for the maddening bowl, he must bring his poison with him. We had found no bread since we left Virginia; we had seen corn-meal and water, slack-baked; we had seen potatoes fried in grease, and bacon encrusted with salt (all thirst provokers), but nothing to drink stronger than buttermilk . . . How can there be mint-juleps (to go into details) without ice? And in summer there is probably not a pound of ice in all the state north of Buncombe County. . . .

[W]e note on all these places departing exceeds the joy of arriving, a merciful provision of nature for people who must keep moving. [We leave in the morning for Valle Crucis.]

THE ATLANTIC MONTHLY:
July, 1885

Valle Crucis
To Cranberry Forge

Next morning out of Boone, on a forest road, we rode through noble growths of oaks, chestnuts, hemlocks, and rhododendrons. The sun shone on our party. I had the pleasure of a school master looking ahead at our group, Starney leading on his black stallion Rebel; Tess on her chestnut Abby, Lily on her Buttercup, The Professor quoting wisdoms, jogging along on his plodding sorrel in front of me. Valle Crucis and Matney proved to be pretty open valleys surrounded by rolling elevations.

We pulled up at a small store with a blacksmith shop. Lily dismounted, went over to look out toward a pretty meadow, came back to sit on the store steps, chin in her two hands. Tess investigated inside, came out to report we can expect no food here. The Professor consulted the blacksmith about a loose shoe, which Starney had pointed out. While they wandered about, I climbed a hill to a white house to negotiate for boiled milk; however, was not tempted to stay in the place.

We heard of a small church to visit, but in blazing sun now, we elected to ride on, no poetry exuding from The Professor, heading for Banner's Elk, eight miles farther. Tonight I will note our honest fatigue but I won't note the silent war between one member and our trailblazer.

The scenery was still lovely but the road steep, stony. We talked out loud about the hope of good food.

Our information took us on to cross a mountain and *pass under Hanging Rock, a conspicuous feature in the landscape and the only outcropping of rock we'd seen, the face of the ledge rounded up into sky, with a green hood on it.*

From this summit we had the first extensive prospect during our journey so far.

Now Lily raised her hand, dismounted, and made her way toward a green space that led up to the rock. We dismounted, too. The high prospect should be a sight to remember and we were willing to rest.

"Something's afoot," The Professor murmured to me. Tess was walking over to Starney, saying whatever she needed to say apparently.

Head down, he nodded and followed the path Lily took. We three watched his slow climb, then the silhouette the two of them made up there. They were not looking at the view.

The Professor did his verse again about love and hate tied in a knot.

I looked to Tess, but the chaperone shook her head to mean to leave them alone. "We're in no rush," she said. "I might as well go to the other side of the mountain for a minute."

We acquiesced to our handy cue for a comfort stop.

Finally Starney and Lily came down, she stalking ahead of him, looking flushed and teary but with her chin up. We asked no questions. In time we all climbed onto our rested horses.

The road was awful, steep, stony, the horses unable to make two miles an hour on it. Now and then we encountered a rude log cabin without barns or outhouses, with but a little patch of feeble corn. Women in the doorways regarding our passage looked tired and frowsy.

We met a happy boy with a good string of quarter-pound trout. He held them up proudly and said he caught them with a hook and a feather tied to resemble a fly.

Finally we reached the residence of Dugger at Banner's Elk to which we had been directed. This had been no dash across country on impatient steeds. We were a weary bunch.

Mr. Dugger did not offer much the pampered child of civilization can eat. A nice fellow, but it was only in the spring house in the glen that we could find short respite to rest awhile. We were not sorry toward sunset to descend along the Elk River toward Cranberry Forge.

The forests grew charming in the cool of the evening as we descended. Whippoorwills sang. Our riders picked up a trot hoping for food and beds at the Iron Company's hotel, a place that may live up to its promise.

First we passed the sights that made the hotel possible — industry in the mountains, forges and iron mines — claiming the land. We rode on above it to alight at the gate of a pretty hotel, crowning a hill. It commanded a pleasing prospect of many gentle green hills, the industry out of sight below.

The cheerful parlor sported novels lying about, and newspapers and fragments of information from the outside world. The ladies, at least, were satisfied and went off to their rooms with the restful feeling they had arrived somewhere, and no unquiet spirit at dawn would say "to horse."

To sleep, perchance to dream of Tatem and his cabin and his household cemetery . . .

Notes at Cranberry Forge . . .

Cranberry Forge is the first wedge of civilization driven into the northwest mountains of North Carolina. A narrow-gauge railway, starting from Johnson City, follows up the narrow gorge of the Toe River and pushes into the heart of the iron mines of Cranberry, where there is a blast furnace, and where a big company store, rows of tenement houses, heaps of slag and refuse ore, interlacing the tracks, raw embankments, denuded hillsides, and a blackened landscape are the signs of a great devastating American enterprise. The Cranberry iron is in great esteem, as it has the peculiar quality of the Swedish iron. There are remains of old iron furnaces lower down the stream, which we passed on our way. The present 'plant' is that of a Philadelphia company, whose enterprise has infused new life into all this region, made it accessible, and spoiled some pretty scenery.

When we alighted, weary, at the gate of the pretty hotel, which crowns a gentle hill and commands a pleasing, evergreen prospect of many gentle hills, a mile or so below the [iron] works and wholly re-moved from all sordid associations, we were at the point of willingness that the whole country be devastated by civilization. In the local imagination this hotel of the [mining] company is a palace of unequaled magnificence, but probably its good-taste, comfort and quiet elegance are not appreciated [by locals] after all. There is this to be said about Philadelphia — and it will go in pleading for it in the Last Day against its monotonous rectangularity and the Babel-like ambition of its Public Building — that wherever its influence extends, there will be found comfortable lodgings and the luxury of an undeniably excellent cuisine. The visible seal that Philadelphia sets on its enterprise all through the South is a good hotel.

This [hotel] has on two sides a wide veranda, set about with easy chairs: cheerful parlors, ... finished in native woods. ... There were, to be sure, novels lying about, and newspapers, fragments of information to be picked up about a world into which the travelers seemed to emerge. ...

The morning was warm . . . and the travelers had nothing better to do than lounge upon the veranda, read feeble ten-cent fictions, and admire the stems of the white birches . . . the rhododendron trees, twenty feet high, which were shaking off their last pink blossoms, and look down into the valley of the Doe. It is not an exciting landscape, nothing bold or specially wild about it, but, restful with the monotony of some of the wooded Pennsylvania hills.

THE ATLANTIC MONTHLY:
August, 1885

In (Dis)Comfort

This morning I found Lily in the sitting room, looking refreshed and pretty, the bouncy hair free of the snood. Yet, she sat quiet and pensive.

She looked up with a question, azure blue eyes wide as an honest child's. "I'm accustomed to comforts at home. But this trip makes me wonder. Is it prideful to dwell on the pleasure of these comforts?"

Aware my sensitivity had already been found inadequate by the lady, I was careful with my response. "Comfort is to be appreciated. And the people who manage to provide it."

"It doesn't make one the arrogant person with false pride, if she appreciates comfort?" She seemed to study her hands, twisting her handkerchief into a knot. "As some people may think of me?"

I ventured, "Is that your own indictment?"

"I must have given that impression to some people, but I'm not like that," Lily protested, but quietly. "If I act like a stuffy, superior Yankee, I don't mean to be, don't want to be taken for that." She sat straighter "Yet a woman shouldn't be charged with self-importance because she has the intelligence to express herself. Oh, I know some girls who seem to talk about manners and fashions as if they think of nothing but the husband they expect to find. I left them back in Newport having their gossipy summer. There are plenty of men who want that kind of wife, to be a pretty appendage."

She looked up to my face as if to a confessor. "Your cousin is that way; that old idea fits in with Alvin's plans, he is all intellectual theories himself, but doesn't expect his wife to have any ideas of her own." Her voice went smaller. "He thinks I'm just that appendage kind of person. But I'm not. For months, I've tried to not let myself see this. Seeing women in other circumstances, and getting insulted by . . . by . . ."

"I know."

"It has made me wonder who I really am. Or who I want to be."

What could I say? She was telling me why she's been indignant with Starney and isn't understood by Alvin. My studious cousin must not be any brighter about women than I am.

"You need some rest," I began. "Travel can test one's notions as well as one's body." I got up, and wandered off to the veranda, a true bachelor coward, telling myself she'll get over this. Cousin Alvin thought this trip would keep her entertained until he was ready to deal with a wife. She's right, Alvin: you don't understand women.

Tess joined me on the veranda, looking refreshed and remarking on the mountain top view.

I asked, "Where is our trailblazer?"

"Outside somewhere looking at the sunset. He's a stubborn young man, carrying old hurts around. At least I understand them now. But you can't change a stubborn man any more than you can move a mountain."

I went off to my room, expecting to find The Professor snoring in pleasure of a good bed. Instead he was poetizing:

> *"Weary with toil, I haste me to my bed,*
> *The dear repose for limbs so travel tired.*
> *But then begins a journey in my head*
> *To work my mind, when body's work's expired."*

I stretched out on my nice bed. "I know what you mean," I said.

Linville Falls Debate

Sunday at the Iron Hotel came up smiling: breakfast was excellent. The ladies of the hotel were gathered in the valley bringing a Sunday school to fifty children from the mountain cabins.

I found The Professor in the sitting room, melted into his chair, reporting, "Everyone is saying we should see Linville Falls. They say it's the most magnificent feature of this region. But I've found no one here who has seen the place."

My experience was the same. A fellow in the kitchen told me he'd never been there himself, and that it was a good twenty-five miles to the Falls over the worst road in the state.

Starney was off seeing to the horses. Lily was absent, too. Tess shrugged at my silent question. The three of us debated: Linville Falls would mean fifty miles and we have already seen some fine waterfalls. We decided to leave Linville to the next explorers. The Roan was unavoidable, however, though I avoided making the point at the time.

Notes upon leaving the Iron Hotel . . .

Toward evening, between showers, [we] rode along the narrow gauge road, down Johnson's Creek, to Roan Station, the point of departure for [our next adventure], ascending Roan Mountain. It was a ride of an hour and a half over a fair road, fringed with rhododendrons nearly blossomless; but at one point on the stream this sturdy shrub had formed a long bower whereunder a table might have been set for a temperance picnic, completely overgrown with wild grape, and still gay with bloom. The habitations along the way were mostly board shanties and mean frame cabins, but the railroad is introducing ambitious architecture here and there in the form of ornamental filigree work on the flimsy houses: ornamentation is apt to precede comfort in our civilization.

Roan Station is on the Doe River (which flows down from Roan Mountain), and is marked at 2650 feet above the sea. . . . The railway from Johnson City, hanging on the edge of the precipices that wall the gorge of the Doe, is counted in this region by the inhabitants as one of the engineering wonders of the world. The tourist is urged by all means to see both it and Linville Falls.

The tourist on horseback, in search of recreation and scenery, is not probably expected to take stock of moral conditions. But this Mitchell County, although it was a Union county during the war and is Republican in politics . . . has had the worst possible reputation. The mountains were hiding places of illicit distilleries; the woods full of grog-shanties, where the inflaming fluid was sold as 'native brandy,' quarrels and neighborhood difficulties were frequent, and the knife and pistol were used on the slightest provocation. Fights arose about boundaries and titles to mica mines, and with revenue officers; and force was the arbiter of all disputes. . . .

The unrestrained license of whiskey and assault and murder had produced a reaction locally in the months previous to our visit. The people had risen up in their indignation and broken up the groggeries. So far as we observed temperance prevails, backed by public opinion. In our whole ride through this mountain region we saw only one or two places where liquor was sold.

It is called twelve miles from Roan Station to Roan Summit. The distance is probably nearer fourteen, and our horses were five hours in walking it.

THE ATLANTIC MONTHLY:
August, 1885

The Roan

We gathered this blithe morning, horses and riders ready to give full indulgence to the spirit of the day — except for The Professor and his reluctance about ascending high mountains.

"It is not with me a matter of feeling, but of principle, not to ascend them," he protested grandly.

Starney pointed out most respectfully, "Roan is a long sprawling ridge. Impossible to go around it, sir, and our trail to Bakersfield leads to the other side."

I reminded the Professor that there was a hotel on top of Roan said to be a famous stopping place. At length, he was obliged to surrender.

Off we went, at an easy pace at first, the road well engineered in easy grades for carriages to reach the top. Only this day it was in poor repair and stony. We had to move slowly through a splendid forest, fine chestnuts and hemlocks. The big timber continued till within a mile and a half of the summit.

There followed a narrow belt of scrubby hardwood, moss-grown, then large balsams that crown the mountain. We come out upon the southern slope to great open spaces, covered with succulent grass. Starney observed, with feeling, it would give excellent pasturage to cattle.

We reined in to look.

"Yes, rich mountain meadows on all the heights here," Starney repeated with obvious pleasure. "When I settle some day . . . " His voice trailed off.

The surface of Roan was uneven, with no one culminating peak, but this afforded various views.

"Have you ever seen such brilliance?" Lily asked. *"Makes every line appear sharply."*

"So peaceful," said Tess.

"Doesn't have the savage aspect of being unsubdue-able as the White Hills of New Hampshire have," The Professor declared.

And Tess: "We are more than 6,000 feet above the sea. It is difficult to believe. Aren't you glad you didn't miss this, The Professor?"

"Strange light up here," he declared.

"That pale look in the sunlight is natural in high altitudes." Starney said. "But look, we have the fog rolling in."

The Professor insisted, "Makes one feel melancholy, the sun withdrawing its warmth and light."

From Lily, breathy with delight, "It's a land of clouds."

"Cloudland, the hotel that's waiting," I said.

The Professor offered a hexameter or two out of Aristophanes, but I declined to pursue the point.

Near the highest points, sheltered from the north by balsams, we found the promised lodging, looking across the great valley to the Black Mountain range.

The hotel proved to be a rude mountain structure, but big enough to offer comfortable rooms, a sitting-room, in which a big wood fire blazed, a true welcome in the evening's 60 degrees.

After dinner, we sat by the fire, attending to talk from the guests, typical of those who come and stay for a time, occupied by mineral and botanical study. Weather was a vital subject. "Mountains create weather. Roan gets some sudden and eerie blows up here. Wind has dug caves here and there on the sides of these slopes."

Later I would regret that Lily missed this information. She and Tess were already in their rooms, and would come out later dressed like ladies.

Notes tonight in the room in a cloud-land setting . . .

The hotel is a rude mountain structure with a couple of comfortable rooms for office and sitting-room in which big wood fires are blazing; for though the thermometer might record 60°, as it did when we arrived, the fire was welcome. Sleeping places partitioned off in the loft above gave the occupants a feeling of camping out, all the conveniences being primitive; and when the wind rose in the night and darkness, and the loose boards rattled and the timbers creaked the sensation was not unlike that of being at sea. The hotel was satisfactorily kept and Southern guests, from as far south as New Orleans, were spending the season there, and not finding time hang heavy on their hands. This statement is perhaps worth more than pages of description as to the character of Roan, . . .

The summer weather is exceedingly uncertain on all these North Carolina Mountains; they are apt at any moment to be enveloped in mist; and it would rather rain on them than not. On the afternoon of our arrival there was fine air and fair weather, but not a clear sky. . . . We could see White Top, in Virginia; Grandfather Mountain, a long serrated range; the twin towers of Linville; and the entire range of the Black Mountains, . . .

The rain was of less annoyance by reason of the delightful company assembled at the hotel . . . [People] thrown on [their] own resources came out uncommonly strong in agreeableness. There was a fiddle in the house, . . . The Professor was enabled to produce anything desired out of the literature of the eighteenth century. What with the repartee of bright women, the big wood fires, reading and chat, there was no dull day or evening on Roan.

THE ATLANTIC MONTHLY:
August, 1885

Second Day On Roan

"How are our ladies doing?" I asked The Professor, interrupting his engrossment in a book. He didn't know if they were enjoying the privacy of their boudoir or out on the summit with Starney.

I admitted my worry and curiosity. "Do you think our Rebel and Yankee conflict has subsided?"

He stroked his beard and contemplated, fired off the aphorism again about love and hate tied in the same knot, and returned to his page.

A lady from Tennessee asked if we had seen anything to compare to Roan Mountain. She thought there could be nothing in the world.

One has to dodge this kind of question in the South not to offend a just local pride. At this mountain place, one could live and be occupied for a long time in mineral and botanical study. Its climate, moisture and great elevation make it unique in this country for the botanist. The variety of plants found here is very wide, we were told, and some rarely found elsewhere. Botanists rave about Roan. The place is satisfactorily kept and Southern guests come to spend weeks or the season.

The grandeur of mountains depends mostly on the state of the atmosphere. After the night of high winds, and foggy morning, a thunder-shower began. Some visitors tried to reach Eagle Cliff two miles off but were driven back by the tempest. Now and then through parted clouds we had a glimpse of mountainside and gleam of a valley. Isolated settlements with wretched cabins evident in the valleys.

Finally, toward evening the sky cleared enough for us to venture out.

Notes from Roan . . .

Towards night, the wind hauled round from the south to the northwest and we went to High Bluff, a point on the north edge, where some rocks are piled up above the evergreens to get a view of the sunset. In every direction the mountains were clear, and a view was obtained of the vast horizon and the hills and lowlands of various states — a continental prospect scarcely anywhere else equaled for variety or distance. Grandfather loomed up more loftily than the day before the giant range of the Blacks asserted itself in grim inaccessibility. We could see a small pyramid on the southwest horizon, King's Mountain in South Carolina estimated to be distant one hundred and fifty miles. To the north Roan falls from this point abruptly and we had, like a map below us, the low country all the way into Virginia. The clouds lay like lakes in the valleys of the lower hills, and in every direction were ranges of mountains wooded to the summits. Off to the west by south lay the Great Smoky Mountains, disputing eminence with the Blacks.

THE ATLANTIC MONTHLY: AUGUST, 1885

The Caves

We were to move on today, but on this foggy morning all seemed unready to leave as if mesmerized by this place. I settled back and duly listened to three women talking of their botany finds. By eleven, winds were up, along with a new torrent of rain.

The Professor and I watched the storm from the windowed parlor, waiting for Tess and Lily to join us for coffee.

Tess appeared looking wide-eyed. "I went back for a nap. Lily wanted to go out for one more mountain top walk. Have you seen her?"

No one had. Everyone stirred about, searching the sitting rooms.

The big cook came out, reporting Starney had left a boy in charge of the horses and shot off running when the rain started. "I ast where he thought he was going, an' he said 'to find a crazy girl'."

Tess, The Professor and the botanist ladies stared at one another and gathered to stare at the heavy gray rain.

I said, keeping down my groan, "They must both be out there. Better together than alone."

The Professor dropped down in a chair, looking pale.

Tess kept to the window, fists tight, staring past the blowing sheets of rain beyond the veranda.

The big cook crooned, "You all can go upstairs and look out all sides." He added, "They's places they can hide until it blows past."

"What kind of places?"

"Places where the wind has plumb dug deep in the sides here and there, like a cave, big enough to hide in."

Five more people stood looking out now, knowing the story and watching weather.

"It's dying down," the little botanist lady announced peacefully. "Wind down, rain easing off. Happens all the time. Another hour and the sun will burn off the fog. Just you wait."

The kitchen fellow brought us cups of hot tea, "I be praying for your folks. We haven't had anybody from here to get plumb blown off the mountain."

At a window, The Professor yelled out like a schoolboy. "Somebody's coming."

We opened the door to the windy veranda. Here came Starney, arms wrapped around Lily, both of them soaked, dragging themselves forward. We welcomed them inside with applause. Their fresh-washed faces looked bright even with their nervous laughs.

Dripping Lily ran one way to her room, leaving soaked Starney standing there panting and breathing hard, long enough to tell Tess, "We found a place to stay out of the worst of it. I'm going to dry out now. Afternoon's going to be clear for going down."

The sky was pink and blue by three o'clock. We five mounted our faithful beasts for departure, *endeavoring to present a dashing and cavalier appearance to the group who were waving goodbye from the hotel.*

In truth, our wanderers turned with regret from the society of leisure to face the wilderness of Mitchell

County. Moving down from Roan on the south side was not as easy as ascending on the north; the road for five miles to the foot of the mountain is merely a river of pebbles, gullied by heavy rains. Besides, we seemed to be keeping thoughts to ourselves.

Bakersville

Our destination was the mountain town of Bakersville, capital of Mitchell Country, eight miles down from the top of Roan.

We rode toward it through silent vast forest, the wind tossing the great branches high overhead as if in response to The Professor's lamenting sonnet, explaining Shakespeare might have had a vision of this vast continent when he wrote:

> *"What is your substance, whereof are you made,*
> *That millions of strange shadows on you tend?"*

Starney called back, "Slow your pace going down."

The valley we finally reached looked fairly thrifty and bright, a pretty place in these hills. We had been told it has six hundred inhabitants, two churches, three indifferent hotels, and a courthouse. Also, the place was said to be favorable to fruit growing and people with weak lungs.

The region's main claim to fame was the mica mining and the exciting possibility of other minerals. Lily saw a sign about gems to be found.

"I want to stop and play in the dirt," she called out.

She wavered between pensive silence and unexpected out- bursts of enthusi- asm since the morning's experi- ence.

We pulled up at an old store for information about the diggings. A local fellow chewing on a pipe told us mica was easily mined but the mines had been dug into for a long time "*maybe by folks before the Indians.*"

The quantity of *refuse, broken and rotten mica, piled up all along the roads, glistened with its silvery scales.* "Some folks have found garnets, yes sir-ee," the fellow added.

Lily turned a longing look down the road at the discarded mica. "I shall find a garnet to keep, as memory of this trip."

"Not I," said Aunt Tess, "I don't care to play in the dirt. Don't you go climbing over that pile by yourself."

Starney spoke up. "If you wanna look for some, I'll go down there with you."

Lily took in a deep breath, without looking at Starney. I hadn't seen the two of them address each other since we left this morning. She started for the small mountains of roadside mica, letting him follow.

I asked Tess, "Have they given up their civil war?"

She shook her head, watching the two. "I think we have a different conflict now. Lily's not talking. How do you like my hat? Bought it inside." She held up a cloth bag edged with ruffles and printed with flowers on a blue ground. When she flipped it around her head and snugged the strings, I saw that it was the sort of bonnet that the local women wear.

Finally, the two came back slowly along the dusty road, the similar sunbonnet Lily had acquired along the way shadowing her face, and Starney's old slouch hat hiding his. Walking up to us, Lily looked up, like a disappointed child.

"No garnets, but the mica itself is beautiful." She displayed a hand-sized fragment framing the delicate image of a fern from the coal age. She tipped it back and forth in her hands, catching the light. "Look. All the colors of the rainbow."

Starney said — kindly I thought, or talking to himself — "You don't expect to pick up the real thing just when you start looking. Maybe it comes up when you've given up looking."

Notes written sitting on a hard bed in Bakersville . . .

Bakersville, the capital of Mitchell County is eight miles from the top of Roan, and the last three miles of the way the horsemen found tolerable going, . . . The valley looked fairly thrifty and bright and was a pleasing introduction to Bakersville, a pretty place in the hills, of some six hundred inhabitants, with two churches, three indifferent hotels and a courthouse. . . .

This is the centre of the mica mining and of considerable excitement about minerals. All around, the hills are spotted with 'diggings.' Most of the mines which yield well show signs of having been worked before, a very long time ago, no doubt by occupants before the Indians. . . . Garnets are often found imbedded in the laminae, . . . It is fascinating material to handle and we amused ourselves by experimenting on the thinness to which its scales could be reduced by splitting. It was at Bakersville that we saw specimens of mica that resembled the delicate tracery of the moss agate, and had the iridescent sheen of rainbow colors . . . . In the texture were the tracings of fossil forms of ferns and the most exquisite and delicate vegetable beauty of the coal age. But the magnet showed this tracery to be iron. We were also shown emeralds and 'diamonds,' picked up in this region, and there is a mild expectation in all the inhabitants of great mineral treasure. . . .

This excitement over mica and other minerals has the usual effect of starting up business and creating bad blood. Fortunes have been made, and lost in riotous living; . . . [L]aw suits about titles and claims led to [quarrels and murders.] Mica and illicit whiskey worked together to make this region one of lawlessness and violence. Perhaps the worst of this is already a thing of the past; for the outrages a year before had reached such a pass that . . . the sale of whiskey was stopped . . . and not a drop of liquor could be bought in Bakersville. . . .

THE ATLANTIC MONTHLY:
August, 1885

On To Burnsville

This morning we rode out of Bakersville, following a small creek the first three miles into the valley. Reaching the Toe River, we had to choose which way to tackle it. *We might ford the Toe at that point, where the river was wide, but shallow, and the crossing safe, and climb over the mountain by a rough but sightly road; or, we could descend the stream by a better road and ford the river at a place rather dangerous to those unfamiliar with it.* Lily, particularly, seemed attracted by the excitement of the danger (perhaps simply to bait Starney), however *we chose the hill road on account of the views.*

We crossed the Toe by a long, diagonal ford, slipping and sliding on round stones.

"Land," cried The Professor as we began to ascend the steep hill, and he went into lines about wishing for a restful death.

At the top the view opened up finely and extensively so that the spirits of us all rose many degrees above The Professor's lamentations. The Professor stopped ventilating his verse, reined in, got off Laura Matilda and trudged up a slope to attack one of a tangle of great bushes of fat, shiny blackberries. I dismounted too, and hailed the others to join us. We began to pick blackberries — Tess and I and The Professor.

A stranger was coming down the trail on a sorrel horse, headed for Bakersville. Starney engaged him in conversation as their horses came abreast, I supposed to extract as much information as possible about the road to Burnsville. They talked a few minutes and the fellow rode on.

I turned my attention back to the blackberries, surprised at my own hunger.

When I looked up again, Tess and the Professor were still busy at the blackberry bushes, and my horse was begging blackberries from Tess.

"Where might the rest of our party be?" I inquired of the chaperone.

Tess shook her head. "Waiting ahead, still in the saddle. They need to talk out these conflicts in private. So I'm picking blackberries."

Before mounting my patient Jack, *I noticed my coat had worked loose from its strap on my saddlebag, the pocket hung open, and my pocket-book was gone.*

Lily and Starney come trotting down the path to check on our delay. I confessed the distressing news.

"That man, the one Starney talked to, just now!" Lily exclaimed.

"No, he couldn't have gotten into the coat. Jack was with me, up in the blackberry patch," Tess said. "He never left my side while the stranger was here."

They knew *The Professor was our cashier, traveling like a Rothschild with large drafts, but I was the sub-treasury and the roll of bills and missing pocket book was a grievous loss. I told them, contrite, "Going back looking for what's lost is a woeful experience, but might we retrace our steps?"*

"It could be lying on the road," Lily said faintly.

"Or in the stream we went through," Tess said.

"What a faithful, understanding party you are!" I said, hopefully.

I'll have to report that losing your funds on a mountain trek adds some excitement the traveler can well do without. But it affords more contact with helpful natives.

All along the way we five walked our horses at a slow gait, looking down and stopping to tell our plight wherever horses were tied to a fence and men sat tilted back in cane chairs on a porch. I told my story with particular inquiries of the man on a sorrel horse headed for Bakersville before us.

Yes, they told me, that would be David Thomas, who had just ridden in. "If he had found it, you will get it back, he's known as an honest man."

The news made a sensation. We dismounted and waited for David Thomas to show up. By the time he did, a crowd of a hundred had gathered, eager for developments.

Mr. Thomas was the least excited of the group as he took his position on the sidewalk, conscious of the dignity of the occasion as if he were about to begin a duel in which both reputation and profit were concerned.

I made my polite speech adding that I've been told if he had found the lost, it was safe as in the bank.

"What sort of pocket book was it?" Thomas asked.

"Of crocodile skin, or was sold for that, and about so large," I said.

"What had it in it?"

"Various things," I answered. "Some specimens of mica; some blank checks."

"Anything else?" went the query, all listening.

"Yes, a photograph. And something that I presume is not in any other pocket in North Carolina — a lock of the hair of George Washington, Father of Our Country."

"How much money?" went David Thomas.

"Perhaps something over a hundred dollars," I answered, staying patient.

David Thomas slowly pulled the loved and lost out of his trousers pocket. "Is this it?"

"It is," I said. Agreeing to his next question, "Yes, I'd swear to it."

The collected audience took a collected breath and watched the counting of the bills and my handing over one of the best engraved notes to David Thomas, who said it was abundant, the crowd agreeing.

I told them, "I am exceedingly grateful to you. Washington's hair is getting scarce and I did not want to lose these few, gray as they are. I will go away with a high opinion of the honesty of Mitchell County."

"Oh, he lives in Yancey," cried someone from the crowd as all watchers laughed.

After that delay, we voted to start afresh in the morning to travel the eighteen miles to Burnsville and handle the Toe again.

A River Guide

$\mathcal{I}$n high spirits this morning we prepared to head again for Burnsville. *We spread the news of our recovered property that afternoon at houses where we had asked. Every man appeared to feel that the honor of the region had been on trial and had stood the test.*

Now to face the eighteen miles to Burnsville.

"There's a mail rider out there who says he can lead us by the shorter route," Starney reported. "I dunno..."

We were saddled up in front of a creaky store, waiting for Tess and Lily, who spotted candy sticks.

The mail rider came up, a *lean, sallow sinewy fellow, riding a sorry-looking sorrel nag.* "Yep. Shorter route, and I can pilot you over the dangerous ford of the Toe, you bet. You folks want me to show you where to ford the Toe?"

We looked at one another, called the two women and set out with the fellow, knowing he exhibited a great deal of ingenuity in endeavoring to excite our alarm as we were paying him a few dollars.

"The Toe gets up sudden," he told us, "folks can get carried away. There's been right smart rain lately. Mebbe you're used to fording? You'll get along if you

mind your eye. Rocks to look out for. But you'll be all right, if you follow me."

Our mail-rider wasn't in a hurry. He glanced past a frowning Professor to Starney in his old blues and grays. "You be a boy in the war? I been *sixteen months, in Hugh White's regiment — reckon you've heerd of him?*"

"I have," Starney snarled, turned on his heel and stalked away.

"What did you do?" The Professor asked.

"Which?"

"What did you do in Hugh White's Regiment?"

"Oh, just cavorted round the mountains."

"You lived on the country?"

"Which?"

"Picked up what you could find, corn, bacon, horses?" the Professor asked.

"That's about so," said he. *"Didn't make much difference which side was 'round, the country got cleaned out."*

The Professor persisted, "Plunder seems to have been the object?"

"Which?"

"You got a living out of farmers?"

"You bet."

Our guide seems to have been a jayhawker, on the "right" side. I could only speculate how Starney might have reacted to this realization, and credited him with great restraint, perhaps on account of his responsibilities to the ladies.

The said ladies joined us, waving small packages of their stick-candy find. Starney reappeared, to give Lily a steady look. "You ready to ford the Toe?"

She stuck her little chin up. "Yes."

"All right," he said with a weariness I had not heard from him before. It sounded like weariness. Or understandable confusion in dealing with a woman.

We took on this local guide who had two trains of ideas running in his mind, the danger of the river, and swapping. *His saddle was a small flat English pad, across which was flung a United States mail pouch, apparently empty,*

"Mine is new," he said, "and yours old so I am open for an exchange as I fancy army saddles."

I told him, "The one I ride belonged to a distinguished Union general and has a bullet in it from Bull Run. I wouldn't part with it for money. And no, I won't give up the rubber coat and leggings."

Off we went. *When we met a yoke of steer, our mail rider turned round and bantered with the owner for a trade. Later, he said, to us, "This hoss of mine is just the kind of brute you want for this country. Your hosses is too heavy. How'll you swap for that one o' yourn?"*

Long before we reached the ford, our riders nodded to one another in silent agreement that we should like to swap the guide, even at the risk of drowning.

The ford was passed in due time with no inconvenience save that of wet boots. The stream was breast high to the horses, broad and swift and full of sunken rocks and slippery stones.

The Professor, lower to the water than the rest of us, Laura Matilda being short-legged, called out, *"This torturous crossing is not one to recommend in your article of information to other hapless adventurers."*

There is a curious delusion for the rider crossing a swift broad stream. It is that he is rapidly drifting up-stream while in fact the tendency of the horse is to go with the current.

The five of us, free of our guide, trotted down the road that led to Burnsville, *a route picturesque with streams and ever-noble forest, past small log cabins, poor structures.* An inn waited ahead, reputedly fine.

Tess sang out, "I have high hopes for a feather bed."

Burnsville, At Last

Burnsville, seat of Yancey County, waited ahead. We trotted into the town's heart, found it to be a square, more like a New England village and inn than any we'd seen.

Lily, who had been quiet along the way, looked pleased. "Auntie, it just might have a feather bed."

We circled around the open square — a shabby courthouse, two small churches, a jail, a couple of stores, and what we were looking for, the recommended mountain lodging place: the Way family inn, fronted by a shaded porch. I, too, wished for the pleasure of a feather bed, though manly attitudes prevented the admission.

At the front desk, *the proprietor turned out to be an intelligent and enterprising man who let us know he had traveled often in the North. He was full of projects for the region and had expanded this place. Floors were painted in alternate stripes of vivid green and red. Our host showed us his collection of minerals and offered to take us to a neighboring hill where we would be able to see Table Mountain to the east and the nearer giant Blacks.*

We made tentative plans, heard about the chimes

that would announce dinner, and we trudged up narrow wood stairs to our rooms.

The gallery between the two long halls looked much like an ante-bellum parlor, complete with a piano made of heavy, ornate mahogany. Lily cried out with pleasure, sat down and caressed the yellow keys. The massive piano emitted plaintive notes, slightly flat.

Starney watched like a nervous stallion in a china shop. I heard him say to Lily, "You do belong in nice parlors with pianos, even if you can handle your horse."

Rather than looking pleased and gratified, she looked up, stricken, and turned back to keys.

Starney moved on down the hall. No sleeping on the front veranda at this place.

In our room, The Professor listened patiently to my repeated self-reproach for not understanding women. He was happy to see the china pitcher of water, towels, and other familiar necessities down the hall. He looked forward to sitting himself in a pretty window seat, with an old magazine he found. "I must feed my soul in comfort to prepare for future physical demands." He hoped the evening would mean a pleasure he'd been missing, since downstairs there had been good aromas from the kitchen.

Notes tonight in this hospitable establishment on the Burnsville square . . .

The county seat of Yancey, at an elevation of 2840 feet, is more like a New England village than any hitherto seen. Most of the houses and buildings stand about a square, which contains the shabby courthouse; around it are two small churches, a jail, an inviting tavern, with a long veranda, and a couple of stores. On an overlooking hill is the seminary. Mica mining is the exciting industry, but it is agriculturally a good country. The tavern had recently been enlarged to meet the demands for entertainment, and is a roomy structure, fresh with paint and only partially organized. [We] travelers were much impressed with the brilliant chambers, the floors of which were surprisingly painted in alternate stripes of vivid green and red. . . . The elevation of Burnsville gives it a delightful summer climate, the gentle undulations of the country are agreeable, the views noble, the air is good and it is altogether a "livable" and attractive place. . . .

But it should be said that before this country can attract and retain travelers, its inhabitants must learn something about the preparation of food. If, for instance, the landlord's wife had traveled with her husband, her table would probably have been more on a level with his knowledge of the world and it would have contained something that the wayfaring man, though a Northerner, could eat. We have been on the point several times in this journey of making the observation, but have been restrained by a reluctance to touch upon politics, that it was no wonder that a people with such a cuisine should have rebelled. [We] travelers were in a rebellious mood most of the time.

THE ATLANTIC MONTHLY: **August, 1885**

On the Square

The Professor and I were taking our repose in rocking chairs on the porch, watching a hot quiet day, with stores closed, the two churches too, as it was not the Sunday for an itinerant preacher. The jail was quiet as no liquor was sold around here. We waited for the chimes to ring for mid-day Sunday dinner.

Chaperone Tess came out looking worried, and claimed a rocking chair before we could stand like the gentlemen we are. "Lily won't get out of bed. She's like a child with the counterpane pulled up, shutting out the world."

"That is what I was afraid of." I regretted saying it aloud.

Tess gave me a reproving stare. "That girl has been wonderful, and you know it. She's managed to stay right up with you old men and our young muscled pathfinder."

The Professor cleared his throat. "Age is not the issue here."

"What is?" I asked, needing to hear the answer.

"It's the girl's heart. And her womanly pride," declared Tess.

"I've seen them talking out of our hearing. Was that more debate or agreement? I thought she and Starney were getting along better." I sensed I was about to find out otherwise.

Tess rocked and shook her head. "My sweet confused Lily says we are to go on without her, but I don't believe for a moment she means that."

I reflected on my old beliefs, proven now, that a man cannot understand how women's emotions are to be deciphered.

The Professor ascribed to no such lack. "The case is clear to me. She has fended off that boy's lack of respect for what he calls privileged, spoiled, Yankee girls. She has protested and proven she can follow him up any trail. Now, you have observed, he is most careful not to offend. Can you tell us why is she so disturbed at this point?"

Tess kept rocking. "I believe she has come upon a fork in the road and she doesn't know which path to take."

We three pondered that.

"Where is Starney now?" I asked. "There go the chimes. That means dinner. Surely Lily will come down?"

Tess shook her head. "I'll have to take something up for her and see if she'll talk." She stood up with deep chest sigh. "Don't you pity the young, with all those feelings, trying to make sense of their lives?"

It was sundown when Starney reappeared.

"What adventure kept you from ham dinner?" The Professor called. "Best we've had here."

Our trail leader dropped into one of the rockers. "Helping out at the jail," he explained briefly without enthusiasm. Two fellows of some local capacity had arrested a young man for carrying a pistol, *not that the boy had shot any-body, but had flourished it about and threatened and the neighbors couldn't stand that.* They wanted to lock him up in the jail, only they couldn't find the key. The jail had been empty for awhile.

The local law explained, *"No use to run a jail if there's no whiskey around."*

The Professor and I exchanged glances and agreed *it's a good thing we had not taken friends' advice and brought along a revolver each. Else we'd be waiting in the Yancey County jail with the young man —* if ever they found the key.

After a quiet rocking moment or two, The Professor cleared his throat like a judge. "Starney, you haven't said what your plans may be once we end this adventure in Asheville. You are back in your South, after all."

Starney's rocker slowed and stopped. He took a long minute to answer, as if to himself. "I'd like my own mountain top, with a valley, maybe, to grow tobacco. I'd like to build a house that celebrates the land it looks out to. I'd have fine horses so people like you visiting could explore the hidden places. I'd want good schoolmarms down a sure road who would teach my children, if I had any. Teach them to know both the good and the wrongs of the world so they wouldn't be taken by surprise."

"So you've done some planning," I said with respect.

The Professor added, "To have those children you'll have to put up with a wife, more's the point, you'll have to find one who wants the same. Maybe one of those school teachers."

"Yessir, I've even imagined that." But it sounded rather sad like a thought he'd given up. He stared out to the darkened square.

The Professor patted his rotund middle. "We're going back in for the pies and coffee. They put it out on the table about this time. The women are upstairs. Want to join us?"

Starney said, "No," and kept on slow rocking.

I went out later to find him gone. Another guest of the house, a sedate, long bearded traveler, and the landlord were in conversation upon a debate well known since Socrates; the pursuit of wealth to the exclusion of noble interests.

"All I want," said the long-bearded one "is enough to be comfortable. I wouldn't have Vanderbilt's wealth if he'd give it to me."

"Nor I," from the other. "I heard tell of a young man who went to Vanderbilt to get employment. Rich fellow asked the young fellow if he would be satisfied with what he, Vanderbilt, got himself. Oh the young one was happy with that. And what did he get? All he could eat and wear. That was the pay the old skinflint gave."

"I declare." The bearded man went on to say, "I hear Vanderbilt's house has a vault built in it where he puts in his gold. And I've heard he's building a mansion right in Asheville. Maybe he has lots of houses."

They went on talking into the night about how the moneymaking spirit showing up in the country would surely destroy the present simplicity.

Notes made tonight in Burnsville . . .

From Burnsville the next point in our route was Asheville, the most considerable city in western North Carolina, a resort of fashion and the capital of Buncombe County. It is distant some forty to forty-five miles, too long a journey for one day over such roads. The easier and common route is by the Ford of Big Ivy, eighteen miles, — the first stopping place; and that was a long ride for the late afternoon when we were in condition to move.

The landlord suggested that we take another route, stay that night on Caney River with Big Tom Wilson ... cross Mt. Mitchell, and go down the valley of the Swannanoa to Asheville. He represented this route as shorter and infinitely more picturesque. There was nothing worth seeing on the Big Ivy way ... [W]hile the horses were saddling, we decided to ride to Big Tom Wilson's. I could not at the time understand, and I cannot now, why the Professor consented. I should hardly dare confess to my fixed purpose to ascend Mt. Mitchell. It was equally fixed in The Professor's mind not to do it. We had not discussed it much. But it is safe to say if he had one well defined purpose on this trip, it was not to climb Mitchell. 'Not,' as he put it,

'Not my own fears, nor the prophetic soul
Of the wide world dreaming on things to come,'

had suggested the possibility that he could do it.

But at the moment the easiest thing to do seemed to be to ride down to Wilson's. When there we could turn across country to the Big Ivy, although, said the landlord, you can ride over Mitchell just as easy as anywhere — a lady rode plumb over the peak of it last week and never got off her horse. You are not obliged to go; at Big Tom's you can go any way you please.

Besides, Big Tom himself weighed in the scale more than Mt. Mitchell, and not to see him was to miss one of the most characteristic productions of the country, a typical backwoodsman, hunter, guide.

THE ATLANTIC MONTHLY:
September, 1885

Leaving Burnsville

Our departure was delayed; Lily still kept her room. We four took our time over a good breakfast — biscuits, honey, eggs, thick coffee — even as we quietly fumed.

"My fault," muttered Starney.

Tess gave me her school teacher look. "You have to go up and get Lily to leave with us."

"I do not venture into young ladies' boudoirs," I protested.

"Oh, for heaven's sake, she's dressed. That is a good sign. You owe it to your cousin; you are responsible for her. Go talk to her."

I climbed the stairs, went down the hall, and knocked on her half-opened door. I found her dressed in her riding clothes, sitting in the window seat. Being patient, I said, "We have an interesting adventure coming up today. And you do want to get to Asheville — our destination — and to see your friend, do you not?"

She looked away. I tried another tack. Acting like the older advisor issuing orders: "You make quite a point of letting us know you are not a spoiled, delicate female, and so far you've proved it. Now . . . "

She gave me a proud look, picked up her carpetbag, grabbed something white drying in the window's sun, stuffed it into the bag and faced me. "Is everyone ready?"

In pleasant sun, we were a quiet crew, riding down Bolling Creek, through pretty broken country, to cross the Caney River, and follow alongside it a few miles to Big Tom Wilson's plantation.

There were little intervals along the river where hay was cut and corn growing, but the region was not much cleared and the stock browsed about the forest. We had been told Wilson is the agent of the New York owner of a tract of some thirteen thousand acres of forest, including the greater portion of Mt. Mitchell — a wilderness well-stocked with bear and deer, full of streams abounding in trout.

Also the playground of rattlesnakes.

With all these attractions, we had learned, Big Tom's life was kept lively by watching for game poachers, and endeavoring to keep out the foraging cattle of the few neighbors. The cattle were not the problem, but those neighbors were when they came around looking for their cattle. Lately they had taken to exploding powder in the streams to kill and harvest the fish.

We rode up on the homestead: an open work stable, an ill-made frame house of two rooms and a kitchen, a veranda in front, a loft and a springhouse in the rear. The chickens and other animals seemed to have free run of the premises.

Neither Big Tom or his wife was at home. We found one of the sons lounging on the veranda, and induced him to put up our horses. A very old lady sat mumbling in the kitchen. An inspection of the premises revealed no one else. In one room were three beds; in the other two beds, and one in the kitchen. On the porch stood a loom with a web in the process.

A bright little girl ran up to tell us, "Paw has gone up to brother's house to see if he could ketch a bear that's been rootin' around in the cornfield night before. I expect he'll be back by dark, 'less he's gone after the bear. We can't tell when he'll come."

The Professor and I watched the action. Starney had gone to see the horses comfortably stabled.

Lily looked around, worried. "Have you seen Aunt Tess? Her back is giving trouble, though she won't tell you."

Lily went off to look for her aunt. We saw the two later, sitting alone on a big stone under a huge oak. Lily was massaging her aunt's broad back.

The Professor said, "Big Tom is a thriving man in the matter of family. Look, here come more boys."

It was nine o'clock: the women were gone to their narrow beds, and Starney to his bedroll on the porch, when *Big Tom arrived. Splendid physique, a man of iron endurance, no doubt. Looking us over, he answered our introductions with a simple greeting. He had been told we were coming. He sat down to attack his supper and talk about the bear.*

He hadn't seen the bear, but judging by its tracks and its sloshing around, "musta been a big one. Set a trap so it won't be long before we have some bear meat."

After his supper, Big Tom was ready to tell more bear stories, so he joined us in our room, an accommodation including feather beds, and walls hung about with all manner of stuffy family clothes. He lighted a fire in the cavern of a fireplace.

The Professor looked around at the wall shadows. "Gives the room a Rembrandt-ish look."

Big Tom had waged a lifelong battle with bears, taken the hide off at least a hundred. "As to deer, can't tell how many I've killed, but never for the sport of it. Now, rattlesnakes, that's different."

"Yep, been in the Confederate army all of sixteen months." I was privately figuring that a man with such bravado must have wrought havoc on the Union army.

"In what rank?" The Professor asked.

"Oh I was a fifer."

Since then, he had been engaged in "lawin' " for years in a long-time feud with a neighbor about a piece of land.

When he finally left us, the fire logs were still glowing, The Professor started snoring and I got out my crumpled paper to write my notes.

Notes on Big Tom Wilson . . .

Big Tom Wilson ... not to see him was to miss one of the most characteristic productions of the country, typical backwoodsman, hunter, guide ...

Neither Big Tom nor his wife was at home [when we arrived.] Sunday seemed to be visiting day, and [we] travelers had met many parties on horseback. . . . Presently a bright little girl, the housekeeper in charge, appeared. She said that her Paw had gone up to her brother's to see if he could ketch a bear that had been rootin' around in the corn-field the night before. She expected him back by sundown — by dark, anyway. 'Les he'd gone after the bear, and then you couldn't tell when he would come. . . .'

As night approached, and no Wilson, there was a good deal of lively and loud conversation about the stock and the chores [among the Wilson boys] in all of which the girl took a leading and intelligent part ... It was time to go down the road and hunt up the cows; the mule had disappeared, and must be found before dark .... It was due to the executive ability of this small girl, after the cows were milked and the mule chased [home], and the boys properly stirred up, that we had supper. It was of the oil cloth table, iron fork, tin spoon, hot bread and honey variety, distinguished, however, from all meals we have endured or enjoyed before by the introduction of fried eggs (as the breakfast next morning was by the presence of chicken), and it was served by the active maid with right hearty good will and genuine hospitable intent.

While it was in progress, after nine o'clock, Big Tom arrived, and, with a simple greeting, sat down and attacked the supper and began to tell about the bear ... Long after we had all gone to bed, we heard Big Tom's voice, through the thin partition that separated us from the kitchen, going on to his little boy about the bear ... The boy was never tired of [it]. And Big Tom was just a big boy also in his delight in it all.

THE ATLANTIC MONTHLY:
September, 1885

Mount Mitchell
On Horseback

This morning, three of us enjoyed the chicken and fried eggs. The chicken was our first on this trip. Starney and Lily were missing.

I gave Tess a level look. "What can you tell us, Madam Chaperone?"

"Don't add to my concerns. I can tell you this: a chaperone must not only watch, but she must know when to be wise and wait. They saddled up early and I did not deem it necessary to follow. I believe they had to talk."

At that point, here came Lily and Starney, marching to the table, exclaiming over the eggs. Their stoic faces and polite smiles were shows for our benefit.

I had to ask the ladies, "Are you willing to do Mt. Mitchell?"

Lily gave me a sweet, unreadable smile. "Hear that brook running so free over stones? Singing, singing as if it doesn't know it's rushing toward a fall down the mountain, a wild, terrible and beautiful mountain. I'm glad I came though I'll be leaving it." She did not explain.

Our immediate problem now was getting The Professor to agree to cross Mt. Mitchell.

Big Tom Wilson walked in and scooped up some biscuits."Going to show you folks the way to go." He had eaten his breakfast hours before.

"Why, the old man," one of the son's confided to me as we prepared our gear for the trek, "can begin and talk right over Mt. Mitchell and all the way back, and never take a break."

Perhaps it was fascination with Big Tom, or the fact that it would save time and we could ride all the way, or the promise of an inn on the other side of Mt. Mitchell that encouraged The Professor, who acquiesced with no protest worth noticing as preparations continued.

We five started off as *Big Tom swung along ahead — on foot — talking nineteen to the dozen. As we rode up the Caney River, we noted a delightful freshness in the air and the smell of this fine open forest.*

We trotted through dew-laden laurel bushes past noisy brooks.

Big Tom barked out; "Ahead we're to stop at Murchinson's hunting shanty, write our names on the wall, that's custom."

As we climbed, husky Tom, full of information, walked along. Starney moved ahead and came back with his warnings. *"There's a very old bridle path up this mountain but it's badly washed, trees fallen across. Means we will have to take long detours to avoid gullies, quaggy places, heaps of brush and rotten logs."*

Starney had warned us early in this trip of the folly of attempting to climb certain slopes by horseback, but to hear Big Tom last night, nothing was physically impossible.

Practical Tess said, "At this point, *it seems as easy to go forward as go back, so we might as well go on."*

Oaks, chestnuts, poplars, hemlocks, all sorts of northern and southern growths met here in splendid array. Such gigantic trees continued two-thirds up the way. Maple, black walnut, buckeye, hickory, the locust, and the largest cherry trees we had ever seen.

Halfway up, Big Tom stopped us to look at his favorite, the biggest tree he knew. A poplar or tulip, it stood there more like a column than a tree, rising high into the air, perhaps sixty to a hundred feet before putting out a limb. In girth, six feet from the ground, it must have been close to thirty-two feet around.

"This giant was here when that fellow Columbus tried to find America," Big Tom said.

The Professor lost his hat trying to look up, had to scramble down off his low Laura Matilda to retrieve it. "We've already seen some that were sprouts when Shakespeare first put pen to paper."

Still higher, we entered a garden of white birches and then a plateau of swamp, thick with raspberry bushes, and finally, the ridges, densely crowded with black balsam.

"I hear no birds," Lily said. "It is primeval silence."

Minutes later, Starney said, "Listen. Humming."

"Bees," offered Big Tom. He pointed upward into the treetops. The upper branches were alive with them. He marked a bee gum to visit later, as honey-hunting is one of his occupations.

We moved on. How rich and fragrant these forests! At the peak, we all voiced inspiration for the sights.

The Professor boomed out like a thespian on a grand stage:

> . . . *Here in the clouds, in the tempests,*
> *Where the lightning plays and the thunders leap*
>   *amid the elemental tumult,*
> *Occasional great calm and silence and*
>   *pale moonlight . . .*

Our female riders murmured about wild beauty, though *the struggle seemed more severe the higher we climbed, with surprising highland marshes, with ever worse footing for the horses. At times it was safest to dismount and lead them, but this was also dangerous for they were likely to tread on our heels in their flounderings in the steep, wet, briar-grown paths.*

At one particularly marshy place, where the wet rock sloped into a bog, Starney thought it wise we dismount, but Big Tom insisted the horses would make it if we but gave them their heads.

The next we knew, Rebel's four heels were in the air, and he came down on his side in a flash. Lily was off Buttercup in an instant. She caught Rebel's reins and drew her bonnet over his eyes and talked soothingly to him as he struggled to his feet. Chaperone Tess simply took up Buttercup's reins and looked on.

Starney fortunately extricated his leg without breaking it, and Rebel scrambled out with a broken shoe. Lily led Buttercup and Tess's Abby around the offending rock as Starney assisted The Professor and The Friend.

I shall have to find a way to include this incident in my notes without naming my cousin's bride-to-be. I must not leave out Big Tom's stories about finding the body of Professor Elisha Mitchell, for whom this mountain is named.

Many hours later, after the day's tremendous experience, we settled at a place known as Widow Patten's. We made the acquaintance of the family there, reviewed our experience, and heard the last story from Big Tom. I'll have to report the man was fresh as any natural shrub we'd seen along the way. If he was fatigued from walking to the summit it didn't check his easy, cheerful flow of talk.

Tess waited to hear the last story, but Lily excused herself and hurried to their room. Aunt announced for her, "She expects to connect with her friend in Asheville tomorrow."

Starney spoke, wryly. "The Boston friend who married a Southerner here. Yes, go see the 'poor girl'."

Lily paused in her retreat, flashed him a dark hurt glance and stalked out.

Notes on Mt. Mitchell . . .

A bridle path was cut years ago, but it has been entirely neglected. It is badly washed, it is stony and muddy, and great trees fallen across it which wholly block the way for horses. At these places long detours are necessary . . . through gullies . . . quaggy places, heaps of brush and rotten logs. Before we were halfway up, we realized the folly of attempting it on horseback; but then to go on seemed as easy as to go back. . . .

What a magnificent forest! Oaks, chestnuts, poplars, hemlocks, . . . and all sorts of northern and southern growths meeting here in splendid array. . . .

We had been preceded all the way by a huge bear. That he was huge, a lunker, a monstrous old varmint, Big Tom knew by the size of his tracks; that he was making the ascent that morning ahead of us, Big Tom knew by the freshness of the trail. We might have come upon him at any moment, he might be found in the Garden, was quite likely to be found in the raspberry patch. That we did not encounter him I am convinced was not the fault of Big Tom but of the bear. . . .

The struggle was more severe as we neared the summit, and the footing was worse for the horses. Occasionally it was safest to dismount and lead them up slippery ascents; but this was also dangerous, for it was difficult to keep them from treading on our heels, in their frantic flounderings, in the steep, wet, narrow, briargrown path. At one uncommonly pokerish place, where the wet rock sloped into a bog, the rider of Jack thought it prudent to dismount, but Big Tom insisted that Jack would, 'make it' all right, only give him his head. . . . The next minute Jack's four heels were in the air, and he came down on his side in a flash. The rider fortunately extricated his leg without losing it, Jack scrambled out with a broken shoe, and the two limped along. It was a wonder that the horses' legs were not broken a dozen times.

As we approached the top, Big Tom pointed out the direction, a half mile away, of a small pond, . . . overlooked by a ledge of rock, where Professor Mitchell lost his life. Big Tom was the guide who found his body. That day as we sat on the summit he gave in great detail the story, the general outline of which is well known.

The first effort to measure the height . . . was made in 1835, by Professor Elisha Mitchell . . . [After much controversy] in order to verify his statement, Professor Mitchell (then in his sixty-fourth year) made a third ascent in June, 1857. He was alone, and went up from the Swannonoa side. He did not return. No anxiety was felt for two or three days, as he was a good mountaineer . . . [but after several days] a search party was formed. Big Tom Wilson was with it. . . . At length Big Tom separated himself from his companions and took a course in accordance with his notion of . . . a man lost in the clouds or the darkness. He soon struck the trail and . . . discovered Mitchell's body lying in a pool at the foot of a rocky precipice some thirty feet high.

Some years afterward, . . . it was resolved to transport the body to the summit of Mt. Mitchell; for the tragic death of the explorer had forever settled in the popular mind the name of the mountain. . . .

To dig a grave in the rock was impracticable, but the loose stones were scraped away to the depth of about a foot or so, the body was deposited, and the stones were replaced over it. It was the original intention to erect a monument, but the enterprise . . . failed at that point. . . . the mountain is his monument. He is alone with its majesty. He is there in the clouds, in the tempests, where the lightnings play and the thunders leap, amid the elemental tumult, in the occasional great calm and silence and the pale sunlight. It is the most majestic, the most lonesome grave on earth.

After a struggle of five hours we emerged from the balsams and briers into a lovely open meadow, of lush clover, timothy, and blue grass. We unsaddled the horses and turned them loose to feed in it. The meadow sloped up to a belt of balsams and firs a steep rocky knob, and climbing that on foot we stood upon the summit of Mitchell at one o'clock. We were none too soon for already the clouds were preparing for what appears to be a daily storm at this season.

The summit [said to be 6,711 feet] is a nearly level spot of some thirty to forty feet in extent either way, with a floor of rock and loose stones. The stunted balsams had been cut away so as to give a view. The sweep of prospect is vast, and we could see the whole horizon except in the direction of Roan, whose long bulk was enveloped in cloud. Portions of six States were in sight, we were told, but that is merely a geographical expression. What we saw, wherever we looked, was an inextricable tumble of mountains, without order or leading line of direction — domes, peaks, ridges, endless and countless, everywhere, some in shadow, some tipped with shafts of sunlight, all wooded and green or black, and all in more softened contours than Northern hills, but still wild, lonesome, terrible. Away in the southwest, lifting themselves up in a gleam of the western sky, the Great Smoky Mountains loomed like a frowning continental fortress, sullen and remote. With Clingman and Gibbs and Holback, peaks near at hand and apparently of equal height, Mitchell seemed only a part and not separate from this mighty congregation of giants.

As we sat there, awed by this presence, the clouds were gathering from various quarters and drifting towards us. We could watch the process of thunderstorms and the manufacture of tempests. I have often noticed on other high mountains how the clouds, forming like genii released from the earth, mount into the upper air, and in masses or torn fragments of mist hurry across the sky as to a rendezvous of witches. This was a different display. These clouds came slowly sailing from the distant horizon, like ships on an aerial voyage. Some were below us, some on our level; they were all in well-defined, distinct masses, molten silver on deck, below trailing rain, and attended on earth by gigantic shadows that moved with them. This strange fleet of battleships, drifted by the shifting currents, was manoeuvring for an engagement. One after another, as they came into range about our peak of observation, they opened fire. Sharp flashes of lightning darted from one to the other; a jet of flame from one leaped across the interval and was buried in the bosom of its adversary; and at every discharge the boom of great guns echoed through the mountains. It was something more than a royal salute to the tomb of the mortal at our feet, for the masses of cloud were rent in the fray, at every discharge the . . . rain was precipitated in increasing torrents, and soon the vast hulks were trailing torn fragments and wreaths of mist, like the shot-away shrouds and sails of ships in battle. Gradually, from this long range practice with single guns and exchange of broadsides, they drifted into closer conflict, rushed together, and we lost sight of individual combatants in the general tumult of this aerial war.

We had barely twenty minutes for our observations . . . and had scarcely left the peak when the clouds enveloped it. We hastened down under the threatening sky to our saddles and our luncheon. Just off the summit, amid the rocks, is a complete arbor of rhododendrons. This cavernous place a Western writer has made the scene of a desperate encounter between Big Tom and a catamount, or American panther. . . . It is an extremely graphic narrative, and is enlivened by the statement that Big Tom had the night before drunk up all the whiskey of the party which had spent the night on the summit. Now Big Tom assured us that the whiskey part of the story was an invention; he was not (which was true) in the habit of using it; if he ever did take any, it would be a drop on Mitchell; in fact, he inquired if we had a flask, he remarked that a taste of it would do him good then and there. We regretted the lack of it in our baggage. But what inclined Big Tom to discredit the story altogether was the fact that he never in his life had a difficulty with a catamount, and never had seen one in these mountains.

THE ATLANTIC MONTHLY:
September, 1885

At Widow Patten's

The Professor and I were in our rooms, in detached quarters; I hoped the women were faring better, though the Widow's roaring fire here made amends for other lacking amenities. *The Widow was highly connected, a member of the Alexander family, and a schoolmate of Senator Vance, "Zeb Vance" he still was to her; and the senator and his wife had stayed at her house.* I speculated that the guest apartments in the main house may have offered the ladies greater comfort.

The Professor stretched his short, solid body on the bed with eloquent groans.

I offered, "You can be proud of experiencing the rare pleasure of today,"

"Alas," he moaned, adding:

"Why didst thou promise such a beauteous day
*   And make me travel forth without my cloak,. . .*
Though thou repent, yet I have still the loss . . . "

"Loss of what?"

"*Loss of self respect. I consented to climb that mountain.*"

"*Nonsense. You'll live to thank me for it, as the best thing you ever did. It's done and over now and you've got it to tell your friends.*"

"*That's the trouble. They'll ask me if I went up Mitchell and I'll have to say I did. My character for consistency is gone. I told them I should refuse. A man cannot afford to lower himself in his own esteem at my time of life.*"

I attempted to distract The Professor from his distress by reminding him of Big Tom. "Did you see how our mountaineer was fresh and still talking, showing no fatigue as we got down?" For he had continued to entertain the company, apparently aware of his reputation.

The Professor added, "He's certainly a favorite with his neighbors but seemed uncomfortable tonight. Do you suppose the social grade here was daunting for our mountaineer friend?"

I speculated that perhaps the reputation of the place might have somewhat impressed Big Tom, though the reality of it, as we had to close the doors to keep out the wandering cows and pigs, and the supper was nothing to brag about, would surely not put his own mountain hospitality to shame.

Now, if I could only rest the body without worrying what had turned our Lily from saucy and independent to quiet and melancholy! Seeing her friend in Asheville might cheer her up. I truly hoped so. I admitted, to myself, that she was a young woman of value. I wished for her happiness and it had nothing to do with the prospect of gaining her as my cousin. Poor Alvin, would he ever understand her?

We soon succumbed to the sleep of peace. Tomorrow we must find a blacksmith for Rebel's broken shoe, then head for Colonel Long's, thence to Asheville.

Notes at Widow Patten's . . .

The Widow Patten's was only an advanced settlement in this narrow valley on the mountain side, but a little group of buildings, a fence, and a gate gave it the air of a place, and it had once been better cared for than it is now. Few travelers pass that way, and the art of entertaining, if it ever existed, is fallen into desuetude. . . . The Widow Patten was highly connected. We were not long in discovering she was an Alexander. She had been a school mate of Senator Vance — 'Zeb Vance' he still was to her — and the senator and his wife had stayed at her house. I wish I could say that the supper, for which we waited til nine o'clock, was as 'highly connected' as the landlady. It was, however, a supper that left its memory.

THE ATLANTIC MONTHLY:
September, 1885

Past Pisgah

he travelers were indebted to the Colonel for a delightful noonday rest and with regret declined the Colonel's pressing invitation to pass the night there on the score that we had two lady riders restless to reach Asheville.

"I for one," Tess said, as we started out riding down a good road from Swannanoa to Asheville. "Am looking forward to fresh clothing."

The Professor agreed, "Ah, yes, one of the true advantages of civilization is the laundress."

"I'm sure. But Lily's friend Emily was kind enough to receive the luggage we sent ahead, so we have things waiting." Tess turned in the saddle just enough to satisfy herself that Lily rode behind her. "You and Emily have a great deal of news to catch up with, don't you?"

"I suppose." Lily answered. She seemed preoccupied with the countryside we rode through. It was pleasant enough, certainly, though The Swannanoa River was here a turbid stream.

Once we arrive in Asheville, our thoughts will doubtless be taken up with its sights, so I shall endeavor to make my notes of this day from the saddle . . .

Colonel Long's is a typical Southern establishment: a white house, or rather three houses, all of one story, built to each other as beehives are set in a row, all porches and galleries. No one at home but the cook, a rotund and broad-faced woman with a merry eye, whose very appearance suggested good cooking and hospitality; the Missis and the children had gone up to the river fishing; the Colonel was somewhere about the place; always was away when he was wanted. Guess he'd take us in, — mighty fine man the Colonel; and she dispatched a child from a cabin in the rear to hunt him up. The Colonel was a great friend of her folks down to Greenville, they visited here. Law, no, she didn't live here. Was just up here spending the summer, for her health. Godforsaken lot of people up here, poor trash. She wouldn't stay here a day but the Colonel was a friend of her folks, the firstest folks in Greenville. Nobody round here she could 'sociate with. She was a Presbyterian, the folks round here mostly Baptists and Methodists. More style about the Presbyterians. Married? No, she hoped not. She didn't want to support no husband. Got 'nuff to do take care of herself. . . . [S]he'd got one child in Greenville, just the prettiest boy ever was, white as anybody. How did she what? Reconcile this . . . with being a Presbyterian? Sho! she liked to carry some religion along; it was mighty handy occasionally, mebbe not all the time. Yes, indeed, she enjoyed her religion.

The Colonel appeared and gave us a most cordial welcome. The fat and merry cook blustered around and prepared a good dinner, memorable for its 'light' bread, the first we had seen since Cranberry. The Colonel is in some sense a public man, having been a mail agent, and a Republican . . . He showed us photographs and engravings of Northern politicians, and had the air of a man who had been in Washington. This was a fine country for any kind of fruit, . . . but it needed a little Northern enterprise to set things going. [We] were indebted to the Colonel for a delightful noonday rest, and with regret declined his pressing invitation to pass the night with him.

THE ATLANTIC MONTHLY:
September, 1885

Asheville

*O*n advice we've been given, for the most impressive view of Asheville, we approached by the way of Beaucatcher Hill, a sharp elevation a mile west of the town. The summit is crowned by a handsome private residence.

From this ridge, the view burst on us. "Captivating," pronounced The Professor, who believes in cities.

"On a variety of levels," agreed Tess, looking at the panorama, then back at Lily and Starney behind us.

We moved on with high expectations.

Notes from the saddle before seeing the town . . .

The pretty town of Asheville is seen to cover a number of elevations gently rising out of the valley, and the valley, a rich agricultural region, well watered and fruitful, is completely inclosed by picturesque hills, some of them rising to the dignity of mountains. The most conspicuous is Mt. Pisgah . . . to the southwest, a pyramid of the Balsam range, at 5,757 feet high. Mt. Pisgah, from its shape, is the most attractive mountain in this region.

The sunset light was falling upon the splendid panorama and softening it. The windows of the town gleamed as if on fire. From the steep slope below came the mingled sounds of children shouting, cattle driven home, and all that hum of life that marks a thickly peopled region preparing for the night. It was the leisure sunset hour of an August afternoon, and Asheville was in all its watering-place gayety, as we reined up at the Swannanoa hotel. A band was playing on the balcony.

THE ATLANTIC MONTHLY:
October, 1885

Pretty Town

The Professor called out with gusto, *"We have reached ice water, barbers, waiters and civilization!"*

On arrival at the hotel, the ladies disappeared toward their rooms. The Professor and I came out to see Starney sauntering down the street.

The band was playing on our Swannanoa hotel balcony. Coming into town from our mountains, the sounds seemed to be offering a predetermined and wilful gaiety. We reasoned this is apt to be presented in a resort, a place where people are intent on finding pleasure.

The late afternoon streets were full of people, wagons, carriages, horsemen, all with a holiday air, *the scene a happy coming together of Southern abandon and Northern wealth, and dashed with African color and humor.*

The Professor declared there was more life and amusement here in five minutes than in five days of what people call scenery. From this I suspected that The Professor must have been brought up in the country.

The shops were open, some very good ones. We did some strolling ourselves and spied a strange sight,

Starney in a shop buying himself a shirt. The hotels promised dancing. On the galleries and in corridors, groups of young people moved about, a little loud in manner and voice.

We observed young gentlemen hat-lifting and bowing to the girls who seem to be here from lesser Southern cities. Blushing or coy, the girls seemed charmingly pleased with the attention.

Back at the Swannanoa, we watched a half a dozen bridal couples, readily recognizable by the perfect air of acting if they had been married a long time.

The Professor and I agreed from our elder, sagacious points of view, they have a large world to find out yet in each other, *such as Columbus never discovered.*

"I still think our Lily's problem is pride," The Professor said. "And a disturbing change of opinions. Their early combat has turned into a different kind of battle of wills."

"She is engaged to my cousin Alvin," I reminded him, or myself. "This excursion was to keep her busy and away from hat-lifting and bowing young men at Newport." Remembering her plaint — "men don't understand" — I gave the old rogue credit for getting nearer the answer than I had.

We come back out of the hotel to a balmy evening.

The band of musicians on our hotel balcony were again scraping and tooting and twanging with a hired air. On the opposite balcony of the Eagle, a rival band echoed and redoubled the sounds. The supplied gaiety was contagious; the horses on the street showed it. They minced and pranced along carrying their riders, including pretty girls adept as Lily in the saddle.

Lily and Aunt Tess joined us on the veranda, looking as if they'd never ridden a dusty trail or rain-swept mountain. Lily was a vision in silk with a lace collar and Tess the proper city matron in a dark suit with ruffles at the throat. They both smelled of roses.

Lily solved the mystery. "Emily was kind enough to have our trunks brought here from the station weeks ago."

I announced, "We've gone through enough travails together. We should investigate what gaiety this resort town offers before you take off tomorrow to visit your friend Emily."

We four stood there on the porch, and considered the night.

Looking up and down the lively street, Lily said in her pert voice, "All five of us should investigate the night, by way of saying goodbye. Auntie and I will stay a fortnight with Emily."

Tess spoke up. "There's Starney over there, getting attention."

Lily's head whipped around. "Where? Who are those girls?"

The Professor did what someone needed to do. He marched across the street, spoke to our trail blazer. Starney followed him back, saying little, but with his brown eyes questioning Lily.

"We thought you'd like to visit around with us," she said, making it sound offhand. "As our goodbye. I'm going on to Emily's tomorrow, Aunt Tess and I, not going back with you three. . . ." Meeting his gaze, she burst out with, "You've wearing a new shirt!"

"I'm in town," he grinned and sobered as quick. "So tonight, that's it?"

The question hung in the air. The band clattered on.

Off we went, five people who did not know how to walk together on a street with other people and horses. So I led, Tess and the Professor following, and the other two, at a slower pace, behind.

I directed us up the round knob of Battery Point to an advertised lawn party. It was a hill with a grove and charming view, fortified during the war, illuminated this night with Chinese lanterns. Little tables were set out about under the trees for the service of cake and ice cream, provided by the Presbyterian Church.

Ladies sitting about at the tables made a charming tableau looking like flower clusters in the lighted grove. Young men sauntered about, bowing and smiling. Our group of five, lately of the forests, sat down to partake of ice cream, and make small observations. Our farewells were still unsaid.

We descended to the Court House Square where a great crowd had collected, black, white and yellow, about a high platform lit up by four glaring torches. A blackened-faced fellow calling himself Happy John bounded up on the platform, joined by Mary, a bright yellow girl.

We five stood at the edge of the jubilant, expectant crowd.

"He's not a real Negro," said Lily. "He's up there pretending to be a stage darkey like a fool. I hate that. I'd think the real ones would hate seeing him do that. Real ones do not act the monkey like that except on a stage."

"That's the act," Starney said. "Look at the sign."

HAPPY JOHN
ONE OF THE SLAVES OF WADE HAMPTON
COME AND SEE HIM!

"Oh yes," exclaimed a bright woman in the crowd, *"Happy John was sure enough one of Wade Hampton's slaves, and he's right good looking when he's not blackened up."*

We stared up at Happy John of the glib tongue and rude wit, playing impudence, deference, and yes, a fool. The crowd, black and white, roared with laughter.

Lily turned again to Starney, looking as if life depended on his answer, "Do you think it's funny to pretend to be stupid so people can laugh at you?"

The Professor threw up his hands. "Let us not start the Yankee-Rebel war again."

Lily waited, adamant. She let him pull her gently away from the noisy folks around us but I heard some of Starney's quiet answer.

"I've seen a lot of places, Lily. And people. And wrongs. It's easier for folks to go along with stupid habits than try out new ones. Don't accuse a whole part of a country by judging the crowd who makes the most noise."

We left the crowd and wandered back to the hotel, most of us silent. If I include any of this incident in my report, I shall have to reflect upon its significance.

The Professor offered a suggestion for our entertainment tomorrow. *A visitor could lounge in the rooms of the hospitable Asheville Club, or he could listen in on a debate between two presidential electors running in that district. At a first debate, the Republican did not show up, and the Democratic orator called his adversary a baboon and a jackass with impunity. The political hit called forth great applause.*

Also, he reported, we could sit on the sidewalk in

front of the hotels and talk with colonels and judges and generals and ex-members of Congress. The talk would generally shift to the new commercial and industrial life of the South, if we wanted to know that. The conversation would also take a reminiscent turn, with a lack of bitterness and tone of friendliness, however, until with studied frowns, they'd get to the "Negro problem." Some would be heartily glad slavery was gone and would talk about the education needs. Others would rant about the scarecrow of "social equality."

"The world is not perfect, for sure." Starney said to the night. "But I've found hate doesn't cure the problems."

"What is a young man's answer?" Tess challenged, huffing along, hand on the arm of silent Lily, as if for comfort.

Starney was silent a minute. "The answer has to be making your own personal choice of who to be, what to believe."

We left those two young people on the dark veranda to say their goodbyes.

I did leave an invitation. "The Professor and I are going to spend some days investigating excursions out of Asheville. So if you change your minds about accompanying us on the return....leave word here."

Notes on an Asheville visit . . .

[My report from Asheville must say there are certain excursions that one can consider.] The sojourner at Asheville can amuse himself very well by walking or driving to the many picturesque points of view about town. Livery stables abound and the roads are good. The Beaucatcher Hill is always attractive. Connolly's, a private place a couple of miles from town, is ideally situated on a slight elevation in the valley commanding the entire circuit of mountains. . . .

Asheville, delightful for situation, on small hills that rise above the French Broad below its confluence with the Swannanoa, is a sort of fourteenth cousin to Saratoga Springs. It has no springs, but lying 2,250 feet above the sea, and in a lovely valley, mountain girt, it has pure atmosphere and an equable climate; and being both a summer and winter resort, it has acquired a watering place air. . . . [T]he scenery is so charming and noble, the drives are so varied, the roads so unusually passable for a Southern country, and the facilities for excursions so good, that Asheville is a favorite resort.

Architecturally, the place is not remarkable, but its surface is so irregular, there are so many acclivities and deep valleys, that improvements can never obliterate that is perforce picturesque. It is interesting also, if not pleasing in its contrasts — the enterprise of taste and money here struggles with the *laissez-faire* of the South. The negro, I suppose, must be regarded as a conservative element; . . . And to say the truth, the new element of Southern smartness lacks the trim thrift the North is familiar with; though the visitor who needs relaxation is not disposed to quarrel with the easy-going terms on which life is taken.

Asheville, it is needless to say, appeared very gay and stimulating to the riders from the wilderness. The Professor, who does not even pretend to patronize Nature had his revenge as we strolled about the streets . . . Immensely entertained by the picturesque contrasts. There were more life and amusement here in five minutes, he declared, than in five days of what people called scenery – the present rage for scenery, any way, being only a fashion and a modern invention. . . .

In the late afternoon the streets were full of people, wagons, carriages, horsemen, all with a holiday air, dashed with African color and humor, . . . peculiar and amusing, a happy coming together, it seemed, of Southern abandon and Northern wealth, though the North was little represented at this season.

As the evening came on, the streets, though wanting gas, were still more animated; the shops were open, some very good ones, and the white and black throng increasing, . . . In the hotels dancing was promised, . . .

Among the attractions of the evening it was difficult to choose. There was a lawn-party advertised at Battery Point, and we walked up to that round knob after dark. It is a hill with a grove, which commands a charming view, and was fortified during the war. We found it illuminated with Chinese lanterns, and little tables set about under the trees, laden with cake and ice-cream, offered a chance to the stranger to contribute money for the benefit of the Presbyterian Church. I'm afraid it was not a profitable entertainment, for the men seemed to have business elsewhere, but the ladies about the tables made charming groups in the lighted grove. Man is a stupid animal at best, or he would not make it so difficult for the womankind to scrape together a little money for charitable purposes. . . .

The evening gayety of the town was well distributed. When we descended to the Court-House Square, a great crowd had collected, black, white, and yellow, about a high platform, upon which four glaring torches lighted up the novel scene, and those who could read might decipher this legend on a standard at the back of the stage:

HAPPY JOHN
ONE OF THE SLAVES OF WADE HAMPTON
COME AND SEE HIM!

Happy John sustained the promise of his name, . . . he had a ready, rude wit, and talked to his audience with a delicious mingling of impudence, deference, and patronage, commenting upon them generally, administering advice and correction in a strain of humor that kept his hearers in a pleased excitement. He handled the banjo and the guitar alternately and talked all the time when he was not singing. . . .

All this, with the moon, the soft summer night, the mixed crowd of darkies and whites, the stump eloquence of Happy John, the singing, the laughter, the flaring torches, made a wild scene. . . .

What impressed us most, however, was . . . the enjoyment of it by all the people of color. . . . I presume none of them analyzed the nature of his infectious gayety, nor thought of the pathos that lay so close to it, in the fact of his recent slavery, and the distinction of being one of Wade Hampton's [slaves], and the menoncholy mirth of

this light-hearted . . . burlesque. . . .

The most sensible view of this whole [negro] question was taken by an intelligent colored man whose brother had been a representative in Congress. 'Social equality,' he said in effect, 'is a humbug. We do not expect it, we do not want it. It does not exist among the blacks themselves. We have our own social degrees and choose our own associates. We simply want the ordinary civil rights under which we can live and make our way in peace and amity. This is necessary for self-respect, and if we do not have self-respect, it is not to be expected that the race can improve. It is [treatment we receive] that hurts' . . .

[Happy John] dismissed the assembly, saying that he had promised the mayor to do so early, because he did not wish to run an opposition to the political meeting goin' on in the court-house. . . .

THE ATLANTIC MONTHLY: **October, 1885**

Farewells

The Professor and I were having mid-morning coffee in the mostly empty dining room, resting up, debating which local entertainment to choose for the day. Or rest our legs on the veranda and watch passing action.

The Professor had chosen to wander down the lively street when Lily found me in the dining room. She came in, clutching something in her hands, came over and sat as I bounced up and back down. Her married lady friend had come into Asheville with her, but was out shopping.

"I have a letter here for Alvin," she said, sounding sad and shaky. "And the bracelet he gave me. I wanted you to know so I'll let you post it with whatever you intend to write. He has a long time over there and is in no hurry, I'd say."

"Would you wish to talk about it?" I asked. "You've left me wondering what exactly has been troubling you."

Her sigh had the sound of frustration. "I know. I had to think it over for myself."

I waited.

"This excursion," she said, looking away, "has made me see so much of life that is so very different from what I knew." Throwing wide her arms for a moment, "As well as vistas that wake the spirit. I have also felt such sadness seeing mountain women who haven't had schools and pretty clothes. But I'm not the kind of person who thinks having advantages makes me superior to others, though I might have sounded unbecomingly arrogant."

"Alvin is all Boston-bred and Harvard-made."

"I don't mean Alvin."

Light began to dawn on this old bachelor. She was ready to explain what I had been trying to ignore. I looked around at the almost empty dining room and back to her intent face.

"When I started this adventure, I might have seemed the uppity female that Starney saw me. Well, I'm still a proud New Englander, but not arrogant and haughty. Not now. Because I am more sure now of what I want and don't want."

She looked me in the face, honest as a beseeching child. "The reason I needed to came along was to get away from my own questions, and forget what I was afraid to admit. About marrying Alvin."

As she paused, I waited.

"Alvin is so ambitious about what he wants to do, he doesn't wonder or ask if I'll fit in. He wants an approving hostess wife. He assumes any lady he asks would be so happy . . . would want it. But not this lady."

I looked at the package and back again at Lily. "You realized -- "

"I don't love him enough to be that false to myself." She gave me an unexpected grin of pure impish pleasure. "Isn't that awful of me?"

"It's fortunate, I'd say, that you found out in time and are candid enough to say so." I found myself smiling because I was convinced that Alvin would be considerably more annoyed than heartbroken.

Her problem was not solved, however. She hid her face in her hands as though she were about to cry.

"Then, Lily, what do you want?"

"A Southern trailblazer who is as stubbornly proud as I am, who unfortunately does not believe I can handle his life. We have been that honest with each other. He thinks I deserve something better. He doesn't have money yet to buy his mountain and horses. We've talked but we come to . . . slippery places . . . and precipices." A shaky laugh. "I have my pride. That's what's been hurting. He loves me too, but he has turned noble and stubborn. He thinks I'll go back to the North and forget all about him."

"So, my dear, what will you do?'

"Go to Virginia with my aunt. She needs help on her farm."

I kept looking for Starney that evening and the next day, to tell him stubbornness is not always noble, and that it blocks out the truth. I hadn't seen him around. The Professor and I plan to take off for more sights before heading north.

Aunt Tess showed up on our last evening in a fresh hat and dress. Lily was visiting her friend Emily, looking in on happily married young love, Tess reported. And what a surprise! Starney had appeared at the friend's place to make sure . . . well, he had been there.

Tess wanted to say her own goodbyes and thanks.

"I joined this trip as a challenge against my next birthday and my back, to be frank. Even if the back gave trouble, I was coming with Lily. She needed this exercise. The girl was in such a private din about marrying your cousin, she had to get her mind off the subject for a while."

"Our trip would do it."

"We both proved ourselves, didn't we? Didn't complain as much as The Professor, that old coot. Tell him goodbye for me."

She paused, looking pleased with herself. "I didn't expect the rest to happen but things do show up in their own time, regardless of one's own plans. The Lord provides if you can handle the rough path getting there. For example . . ."

She leaned back, smoothing out her new Asheville muslin. "My farm has become too much for me. Haven't found anyone that I trust to take on its management. It's costly to have an employee just to look after things while I'm gone. Yet I have no intention of selling what I've built up. My horse farm is my home and my life."

"And Lily wants to live there with you."

"I've said yes, though she can't do all a foreman should. I've needed a horse person and farm manager for five years. Now I've got one. The fellow applied; that's the good part. Starney came to me yesterday asking for the job." She chuckled. "We thought he'd gone. No, he was looking in the stores for a garnet for Lily. Think of that."

"You've hired him to go back with you and Lily."

"He swallowed his pride to came asking for the job, which means asking for Lily. He's confided to me that he'll show up the morning before Lily and I start out. Going to deliver some bossy trailblazer instructions. Then hand her the garnet. We might look for a church on the way." She leaned back smiling. "Imagine. I'll have a Rebel-and-Yankee couple taking over, with equally stubborn minds. Should be interesting."

I smiled at her. " Tess, I must send this account to ATLANTIC MONTHLY — but I will edit it strictly. Only we five will know the best of it."

The End

Paul Zipperlin, a life-time artist, of Banner Elk, NC, and Florida's west coast, can produce storytelling characters when called on, but his main love is to paint the natural wildlife of North Carolina and Florida. Impressionism with a touch of realism identifies his work, which can be seen in a number of galleries and fine restaurants. His serious paintings also tell a story. He can be contacted at the Artists Studio Gallery and School in Matney, NC.

Marian Coe (Zipperlin)'s second career following her newspaper years has produced six books, five of them with awards and currently available, with *Once Upon a Different Time* now making the fifth in print. Marian's enjoyable fiction is well reviewed for storytelling that delivers a sense of place, underlying meaning, and believable characters that drive it all.

High Country Publishers, Ltd

invites you to our website to learn more about Marian Coe and her work. Read reviews and readers' comments. Link to Marian Coe's site and find out about her other works and her husband Paul Zipperlin's artwork. Learn what's new at High Country Publishers. Link to other authors' sites, preview upcoming titles, and find out how you can order books at a discount for your group or organization.

www.highcountrypublishers.com

High Country Publishers, Ltd

Boone, NC
2004

Appalachian titles from
High Country Publishers, Ltd.

Where the Water-Dogs Laughed
by Charles F. Price
Fourth book in the award-winning Hiwassee saga
ISBN: 1932158502, $24.95

Appalachian Paradise
by Maggie Bishop
An unlikely romance on a five-day hike in the heart of the Appalachians
ISBN: 0971304564, $9.95

Dear Mouse . . .
by schuyler kaufman
Murder and love on an Appalachian movie set
ISBN: 0971304521, $14.95

Monteith's Mountains
by Skip Brooks
A serial killer chase set in the Great Smokies of 1900
ISBN: 0971304548, $21.95

Plumb Full of History
by Donna Akers Warmuth
A fictional tour of Abingdon, Virginia for the whole family
ISBN: 1932158782, $9.95

Strike a Golden Chord
by Lila Hopkins
Romantic suspense with a Christian orientation with illustrations by the author
ISBN: 1932158510, $23.95

Weave Me a Song
by Lila Hopkins
A heartwarming story of unconditional love with illustrations by the author
ISBN: 0971304572, $19.95

High Country Publishers invite you to order books from our Appalachian series for gifts or for your own enjoyment. You may photocopy this page or simply send a letter or e-mail with the following information to our office.

Shipping address:
Name:
Address
City, State, Zip

____ *Once Upon a Different Time*, $12.95   Total: $ _____
Other Titles:

_____   Total: $ _____

_____   Total: $ _____

_____   Total: $ _____

Tax (.075% only in NC) $ _____
Shipping $3.00   3.00

Total $_____

You may enclose a personal check for the total, or send your credit card information below:
(   ) VISA (   ) Mastercard

Card # _____ _____ _____ _____
Expiration:

Signature:

High Country Publishers, Ltd
197 New Market Center #135
Boone, NC 28607
(828) 297-7127
fax: (828) 262-1973
www.highcountrypublishers.com
sales@highcountrypublishers.com